I0552281

The Hawk and the Wolf

Children of the Wild, Volume 4

Prudence MacLeod

Published by Prudence MacLeod, 2024.

THE HAWK AND THE WOLF

First edition. February 24, 2024.

Copyright © 2024 Prudence MacLeod.

ISBN: 978-1927478653

Written by Prudence MacLeod.

The Hawk and Wolf

by

Prudence MacLeod

Mystery and Mayhem

The door to the lab swung open and another student rushed in. "You're late," said a voice that he ignored. "Bring me that box over there, help me get it open."

"It's heavy ..."

"Don't drop it." There was a sudden explosion as the box hit the floor, and a green dust settled over everyone and everything amid the screams of the injured.

TWO MEN STOOD SILENTLY gazing at the mayhem and destruction that lay before them, separated from it only by a thin sheet of glass. This had been a government lab, a room where people in lab coats poked at this and that, and then wrote notes on clip boards. What could have happened to cause this?

The place was shattered, everything broken and thrown around as though a cyclone had gone through the room. Also, bits and pieces of human and animal flesh were scattered around, and that's what had them both fighting to keep from losing their last meal.

They could see clearly that several pieces of the dead were a mix of animal and human remains, fused together as though some mad god had tried to make new creatures by meshing them together, but failed. Many had obviously been torn apart.

"Sir?"

"Jesus, Egan, what the hell happened here?"

"We don't know, sir, but we've sealed off the building. Only a handful of people have seen this and two are dead already."

"Excuse me?"

"That green dust all over everything, sir. Apparently, it's highly toxic. Director Compton, what do you want to do here?"

The tall, thin, man sighed deeply then turned away from the glass that separated them from the destroyed lab. A tight feeling in his gut told him the choices here would be bad and worse. A slight pain in his chest was ignored as he replied to his companion.

"I want this explained in a way I can convince the senate committee that's it's all a natural occurrence. Hell, I want someone to convince me it's a natural occurrence, not an attack by some foreign power, aliens from space, or demons from hell. Once I have that, I want it all to go away.

"Put the special team on it immediately."

"I tried, sir. Two agents refused to touch it and three others quit. The psychic checked himself into a locked ward. Sir, that green dust, it does something to the mind as well as the body."

"Dammit, we've got to keep a lid on this. We can't let the media or the public get wind of it. All right, I'm wide open to suggestions here."

"Sir, you know what you have to do. There's only one man who ..."

"Oh no, there's no way in hell I'm letting him or any of those people ..."

"Sir, I honestly can't see another option, unless you want to call in the military ..."

"No, no military, no EPA, no disease control ... Ah, shit, as badly as I hate to admit it, you're right. There's only one man capable of dealing with this and keeping it under the radar. I'll make the call."

They walked outside and locked the building behind them. With sagging shoulders, he leaned against the car and pulled out his phone. A moment later he sighed deeply and tossed the phone onto the seat of the car.

"Nothing. The bastard has changed his phone to an unlisted number. All right, keep a lid on this and track him down for me."

"Yes, sir. Sir, what do you think will happen if we can't find him?"

"Then we're screwed. Come on, he's a private eye, P.I.s need work, he can't be that damned hard to find."

AS THE TWO MEN CLIMBED back into the car and drove off, a thin, stooped, woman hurried away, clutching the scarf around her face tightly. She crawled into her own car and, struggling with her misshapen clawed hands, managed to get the key into the ignition and start the engine. She'd heard every word the men had spoken, and although she had no idea who would be coming after her, she didn't want to be found. Not like this.

She drove slowly, carefully, out of the city and into the hill country beyond. She had to find a place to hide. She'd give it a few days, then return to the site of the first accident. Perhaps she'd find an answer there, she had to find an answer.

A few days later, she reached the original sight, the place where it had all begun. It had been cleaned up and there was nothing there except dust and dirt, a discarded cigarette pack and a beer can. A woman she'd worked with had disappeared from this spot months before, only her clothes were left behind. It was ruled a kidnapping by slavers, but she didn't believe it, not now. There'd been hawk feathers found at this site. Somewhere out there was another maddened creature like herself. Somehow she had to find her.

She wouldn't find her though, the woman she sought was far away, hunting.

WHILE A FRIGHTENED and injured woman sought her former colleague, far away a wolf raced through an open field, zig-zagging as he fled. Above, a hunting hawk marked his path and the pattern of his evasive maneuvers. Suddenly, she folded her wings and stooped.

The hawk plummeted towards the ground, unfurling her wings at the last moment, and reaching for the wolf with her talons. She managed to touch his tail, but no more. She spiraled back into the clear blue sky as the wolf turned and ran back across the field.

He changed his pattern as he fled, but she marked him and again fell from the sky. Just as her talons reached for him the wolf turned in mid stride, reaching for her with powerful jaws. The hawk banked, turning in mid-air, causing the wolf to miss. Her wing gave him a buffet on the head as she climbed to high for him to reach.

The wolf stood watching as she returned to the air, lying lazily on an updraft high overhead. With lightning speed, he turned and raced toward the farmhouse in the distance and the barn just beyond. There was no evasion this time, just unbelievable speed.

A few beats of her wings and the hawk was ahead of him, diving toward the barn door below. As the hawk reached the ground she morphed into a naked woman. Her laugh of victory turned to a shriek as the wolf leaped at her. She ducked low and he transformed into a young man as his body passed above her. A forward roll brought him back to his feet in time for a bathrobe to settle over his head.

"Put your robe on before you scare Bill's chickens." The woman was grinning at him, and he was besotted all over again.

Shyly, he tied the robe and turned away so she couldn't see him blush. "That was fun, sweet Ronni. A good workout, too."

"Yes, it was, Igor. Yes, it was. We should probably be getting back now."

"Soon, my pretty bird. First, Igor has to catch his breath. You've worn me out. You've got me ruined."

She laughed at that and gave him a smile that fairly melted his young knees. "All right, let's see if Bill has any coffee brewing. Suddenly I'm hungry."

"Hungry? Why didn't you eat something? There were lots of mice in the field."

Laughing, she cuffed his shoulder then playfully poked him in the ribs to make him flinch. They reached the house to be invited in for coffee. "What's wrong, Bill? You seem a bit distracted."

Bill Walker was the Lair's lookout and resident farmer. "Oh, sorry, Ronni," he replied, as he passed her a mug of coffee. "It's that jersey cow, she's not doing too good. I was up half the night with her. Could you take a look for me?"

"Of course. Igor, would you be a sweetheart and go fetch my bag?"

"Anything for such a beautiful woman." He gulped down his coffee then stepped outside, morphed into the wolf, and raced away toward the mansion in the distance as the bathrobe settled to the ground. Fifteen minutes later a jeep stopped in the farmyard and the young man hopped out, her medical bag in hand. He tossed her a t-shirt and jeans, then followed the old man into the barn. Dr. Rhonda Stockman, also known as Lady Hawk, veterinarian, was close behind.

Much later that evening, a tired vet leaned against the young man's shoulder. "You okay, sweet Ronni?"

"Just tired, Igor. The cow will be fine now, but I need to sleep for a few days. How about you?"

"Da, I'm tired, but I like this."

"This?"

"Sitting under the stars with a beautiful woman leaning on my shoulder. Life is good to me."

She laughed at that. She berated herself for how much she loved being in this young werewolf's company. He was barely out of his teens, and she was nearing thirty. Still, she couldn't seem to help herself, nor did she really want to. "You won't think it so great if I start to snore."

"Stop now, you're spoiling my illusions. Sweet Ronni, I can feel the fatigue in your body. You need to eat then get some rest. Come, let us go back and raid Elaine's kitchen."

"Yeah, we should get back. So, wolf or walk?"

"Ride in style, beautiful lady. I stole Eric's jeep, remember? Come, court physician, your chariot awaits." He rose and offered his hand. She took it and let him help her to rise. Together they walked hand in hand back to the jeep.

TWO DAYS PASSED BEFORE the agent reported back to the director that he'd tracked down a phone number for the missing former agent. "You sure this is the right number, Egan?"

"Yes, sir. He's up north, working for some paranoid recluse on full retainer. Sir, you may have to reactivate him to get him to take on this one."

"Yeah, well, I'm not so sure I want to go there. I'll try bullshit first. Wish me luck."

"Good luck, and may God have mercy on us all if anyone ever finds out what Sawchuk was up to for the last couple of years before he quit." He sank into a chair as his boss dialed the phone.

SEVERAL PEOPLE SAT around a long table, chatting, and just enjoying the day. A powerfully built man furrowed his brow as he looked at his ringing phone. "Director Compton, what the hell does he want? Sire?"

The vampire king nodded his head and Terry Sawchuk answered his phone on speaker. "Director Compton, what can I do for you today?"

"To start with, Sawchuk, you can take me off speaker."

"No can do. Got my hands in muck. We're alone, you can speak freely."

"We'd better be. Look, Sawchuk, I'll get right to the point. We've got a case that's right up your alley. Totally weird shit, lots of blood and gore. Just the way you like it."

"And your own people are completely lost. You need this kept under the radar. Sorry, but I'm on retainer full time. Can't do it."

Suddenly the queen leaned over and whispered softly in Terry's ear. He nodded as the man on the phone went on. "Look, I don't give two shits about your retainer. If I have to, I'll reactivate you and ..."

"Oh, cut the bullshit," said Terry. "You're desperate, I get that. Your people can't, or won't, deal with it. Fine, I'll have a look.

"Here's how this'll work. I'll come look it over, and if I'm interested you'll provide me with a badge for myself and each of my team, as well as full access to all information concerning the case. If I take the case, I work independently and make the whole thing go away, no actual files turned in, no expenses turned in, and no actual reports turned in. Our fee is half a million. Two hundred fifty thousand up front and the rest when it's done."

"Jesus Christ, I can't justify that kind of expenditure without ..."

"Relax, we'll provide you with a plausible story to tell congress, give you a paper report they'll believe, and supporting docs to go with it."

"And not a goddamned word of it will be the truth."

"Forgive me, Director Compton, but if you wanted the truth you wouldn't have come to me in the first place, and we both know that. Oh, I'll need a fully equipped mobile lab."

"All right, Sawchuk, but don't screw this up. You're going to Boone, North Carolina, someone will meet you and your team there."

"So, has Egan Bridger been there?"

"Yes, the deputy director has been there, he'll meet you at the site. I'll e-mail you all the pertinent information."

"He's got to be in the room with you. Egan, what the hell am I looking at here?"

"Dammed if I know, Terry. It's ugly, messy, and right out of a bad horror movie. Philadelphia Experiment type of shit, only worse. Only bring team members with strong stomachs."

"Understood. See you there." He broke the connection then sighed. "All right, Sally, why did you want me to take this thing on?"

"Terry, I have a feeling this is something we should be looking into, not the government."

"You're thinking non-humans?"

"I'm getting a sense of that, yes." Queen Sally's psychic abilities had grown stronger over the past two years. These days her people acted on her hunches as though they were solid fact.

"Okay then, guess I should pick a team and hit the road. Sire?"

"Take whoever you need, Terry."

"Well. Since I have no idea what the heck I'll be facing, I'd like to wait until I get the information. I ..." His phone buzzed again. "Ah, here we go now. Tommy, want to pop this up onto the big screen so we can get a good look at it?" He tossed the phone to his friend who caught it easily. A moment later the big screen came alive with the photos taken by those who had discovered the accident.

"Wow, holy crap," mutter Terry. "Clara, can you make any sense of that?" The small woman rose and stepped closer to the screen.

"Oh my God," gasped another woman at the table.

"Ronni, what is it?" asked the queen.

"My queen, that's the lab I worked out of. I know that woman right there. Oh dear gods..." She was suddenly wrapped up in the queen's arms. Sally cooed soothing sounds for a moment then the woman relaxed. "I'm okay, I am. Thanks, Sally."

Clara Bynes, the resident crime scene investigator, and inventor, scanned the pictures carefully. "Ronni, how many people worked there?"

"At least ten, could be up to twenty on a given day, why, Clara?"

"Because I see evidence of only four here," she replied. "Five at most."

"Any idea what happened to them?" asked King Harald.

"I think I might," Clara replied. "Sire, when Ronni came to us, she spoke of what happened to change her. Ronni, that green dust we see here, is that like what you saw at the time of the change?"

"Could be, that's for sure. Why?"

"Because I think the people who investigated your disappearance took as much as they could of that dust to the lab. That would be a natural if they couldn't readily identify it. I think they took it back and, although it lay dormant for months, something triggered it. See here, there's body parts of lab animals fused to humans, rats, dogs, raccoons, etc.

"For some reason the changes didn't complete. They must have freaked out and tore each other apart. Now, in this picture, the lab door is wide open, that tells me several people escaped."

"Clara, what are you saying?"

"Sire, we could easily have a half dozen changlings, or people caught partway through a change, running loose in that area, maybe more. There could also be people who've turned into mindless creatures made up of several animals. I'd like to be on your team, Terry. I might be able to learn more from that lab."

"I want to go too," said Ronni. "I know a lot of those folks, and I know the area somewhat."

"I should go," said young Igor, as he stood up and looked from Ronni and then to King Harald and back again to Ronni. "You'll need someone who can track them through the forest, yes?"

Ella West, the group's matriarch and eldest of the vampires rose to speak. "I think perhaps that's a job for me."

Ronni's face had begun to redden as Igor gazed at her. She was grateful his attention had been diverted. Silently she fought the attraction to him.

"No, no, Great Mother," grinned the young man. "These people are already frightened. The saber-toothed tiger will just make that worse. A wolf is a more familiar animal and won't frighten them so badly."

"He's got you there, Mother," grinned the king.

The young fellow gulped as the tall elegant woman reached out to grasp his shoulder tightly. "Igor, I'll concede the point to you, but you must listen to me now. We've fought shoulder to shoulder before, and I hope we can do that again one day. I want your solemn promise you'll be extremely careful. No one but the team must ever see you change."

"I understand, Great Mother. The mission is not a place for play. I'll be careful."

"And obey Terry instantly, he'll be the alpha on this mission. Do you understand?"

"Yes, ma'am, I understand."

She didn't like it, but she relented and patted his shoulder then sat back in her chair.

"Who else will you need, Terry?" asked the king.

"I'll need Kylie's urban tracking skills in case some of these folks are hiding out in the cities, and maybe Clyde in case we have to have to talk one down first, or need a profile to work with. Now, here's the big one. Sire, what's the objective here?"

All eyes turned to the king as he sighed and gave that some serious thought. "In a perfect world, you would locate and bring all non-humans here; however, we rarely get a perfect world. Your call, Terry. If you can't bring some of them, or if you judge them to be too dangerous, do what you must. Just make certain no evidence of a non-human can be found."

"Understood, sire."

"You'll need a vampire on your team too," grinned Gudrun, Terry's wife. "Someone who can use the compulsion would be handy, don't you think? Ronni can't do it, neither can Igor."

"You're absolutely right, my love," replied Terry, as he smiled warmly at her, his eyes twinkling with mischief. "Do you think your buddy Marlene might have a few days to spare?"

Gudrun laughed at his teasing. "You'll never tear her away from her girlfriend, Lilly, for that long. However, I think I can make room in my schedule."

"Then my life is blessed," he grinned.

"Terry, take the plane."

"Yes, Sire, can I keep Eric with us as well? The man's got mad skills." The king nodded. "All right team, gather what you'll need. We'll leave first thing tomorrow."

RHONDA STOCKMAN WAS gazing out the window when Elaine arrived with a suitcase. Once again, she found herself feeling grateful for Elaine's kindness and efficiency. "Little wonder the king was happy to have her in his service," she thought, as she packed the small case. She didn't have a lot to put in it..." As she made her few choices, her mind in turmoil, a knock sounded at her door.

"Come in."

"Hi, Ronni, got a few minutes?"

"Clara, sure, come in, sit." These two had almost instantly become friends upon Rhonda's arrival at the Lair. "What's on your mind?"

"You are," Clara smiled. "First, let me tell you again how happy I am that you're here. I'm not a medical doctor, and having a full-fledged veterinarian is such a relief to me. I'm also learning plenty of new and interesting stuff from you, and I like that."

"But?"

"There's no but, girlfriend, not one. Now, here's what's on my mind. It's the green shit, as Terry calls it. First it changed Ella into a saber-toothed tiger, then Torvil into the cave bear, then you into the hawk, and now this disaster in your old lab. We can assume there was some sort of meteor shower back in Ella's day, right? That meteor shower left some small pieces of the toxic stone behind. Some pieces of it are still out there somewhere."

"I'm with you," Ronni nodded.

"Okay, first Ella, next came Torvil, and then you. In each case, there were several common factors. First, the person to be changed was in a "flight or fight" situation, lots of adrenaline."

"Okay..."

"Second, the green shit in each instance came from an exploded chunk of meteorite. Ella's fell from the sky and exploded on impact, Torvil's took a mighty blow from the giant bear, and your stone exploded from a strong electrical charge."

"So, the meteorite needs a stimulus, an explosion or impact of some kind, to activate a full change. The folks in the lab were relaxed and all they had was the dust, not a full stone to activate. Hence, only partial changes?"

"That was my thought, Ronni," said Clara, as she adjusted the glasses on her nose. "I wanted to run it past you first before bringing it to the team."

Rhonda sat on the edge of the bed beside her friend. "It makes sense to me, Clara. I say we go with that theory until we learn different. However, I still want a hazmat suit before I touch that stuff."

"Oh yeah, count on that." Clara continued to regard Ronni with concern. Ronni reached out and lightly touched her friend's hand.

"So, what else about me is bugging you?"

"Ronni, you disappeared from that place months ago. All those people would have found of you would be your clothes. What are we going to tell them when you suddenly reappear?"

"Shit, I hadn't thought of that. Any suggestions?"

"Well, again I wanted to run it past you first, in case you had a plan, but I was thinking this is a job for Terry and Kylie. They can come up with a story and Gudrun can make sure any skeptics believe it." The concern on Clara's face had not relented. Ronni felt her own beginning to rise.

"Okay, that works for me, now tell me the rest of it."

Clara sighed again and looked at her hands. "I've been studying your DNA," she admitted softly.

"And?"

"I've found something strange quite active in it. I've only ever seen it before in Torvil and the vampires. The werewolves don't have that active marker."

"Clara, what are you trying to tell me here?"

"I believe you're immortal, like the vampires. You'll never grow old, you'll revive if killed, and all injuries will heal at super speed."

Rhonda swallowed hard and looked at her friend with wide eyes. "Are you certain? Of course, you are, or you wouldn't have said anything. Wow. Holy shit. Wow. So, now what am I supposed to do? Clara, why did you even tell me this?"

"I don't have a lot of friends. None actually, at least none I felt strongly about until you started taking over half my lab. Ronni, I had to tell you, you deserve to know. Also, time itself will begin to tell you the same thing. The world will change and so will all the people around you ..."

"But I won't. Oh crap, what ...?" Overwhelmed, she looked away as she tried to process what she'd just been told.

Clara reached out and clasped Ronni's hands. "Talk to Torvil, talk to Ella, the other vampires. Ronni, they'll be able to help you adjust as time passes without you."

"Gods, Clara, immortal? I..," words failed her, and she squeezed Clara's hands tightly.

"Just don't make fun of me when I start getting gray hair and wrinkles."

Rhonda chuckled and gave her a friendly nudge. Her face then became serious for a moment. "Tell me, did the meteorite implant the DNA or does everybody have it, and the stone just activated it somehow?"

"We've all got it, but it's dormant."

"Then I have to find a way to activate it," Ronni announced.

Clara laughed. "Yes, well, good luck on that one. Now, before you start that, we have to accompany Terry and gang to sort your former lab partners. You want to borrow that denim skirt again?"

"Oh yes, can I?" Ronni smiled. She was glad to have a friend like Clara.

"I'll ask Elaine to bring it up shortly," smiled Clara, as she rose to go. She patted Rhonda on her shoulder then left the room. A few minutes later, Elaine returned with Clara's skirt. Ronni thanked her and closed the door as she left again.

"I will find a way to activate that DNA, Clara. You're the sister I never had, and if you think I'm living for millions of years without my best friend, you've got another think coming."

She was still mulling it all over in her mind as she drifted off to a troubled sleep. Most people would be thrilled to learn they were immortal, never thinking about the long-term consequences. Rhonda wasn't most people. She planned to figure it out, use the formula on Clara then destroy it utterly. She'd dare not allow it out into the world at large.

And there was something else she had to figure out. Young Igor was barely twenty, but for some reason he set her hormones racing, making her act like a horny teenager, giggling, blushing, and the works. What the hell was up with that?

IGOR WAS PACKING A rucksack when he felt another in the room with him. He turned to see Ella standing in the doorway and gestured for her to enter. "Miss Ella, I know you think I should stay behind, that I'm too young and, what is that word, immature?"

"No, Igor, I don't see you as immature, not anymore." She walked across the room and sat on the edge of the bed. "That time has passed for you. Perhaps had Stephan Krebs not stolen your childhood, I might think so, but not as things are now. No, it's your emerging alpha nature that concerns me now."

Igor tensed at the sound of that name being spoken aloud. He shifted his body weight as he forced those memories back where they belonged.

"Igor, I sense the alpha nature awakening in you, and I can see you holding it back by using humor and playfulness. How long do you think this will work?" The Great Mother searched his eyes for answers, sensing his unease.

"Da, I know." He sat beside her and sighed. "Miss Ella, I won't let the alpha instincts take control of me. If I learned anything at that prison camp, it was how to control my true nature. I know the needs and urges of the alpha are strong, but Igor is stronger," he said, now looking directly into the matriarch's piercing gaze, "I won't fail you."

Ella smiled and gently hugged his shoulders. "You've grown into a fine young man, Igor. I firmly believe you're right, you're stronger than the nature that drives you. This is how we survive, Igor, we non-humans. We use what we are to our advantage, we do not let it use us. Remember."

"I'll remember, Great Mother. You've taught me so much in the past few years, I won't forget the lessons." Igor truly did regard this unusual immortal as a mother, not just to him but to everyone at the Lair.

"I know," Ella smiled, "I just wanted to be with you when the alpha fully awakens for the first time. I'm just worrying. You're one of my own children now, every bit as much as one of the vampires."

"I'm honored that you see me this way. I swear I won't disappoint you."

"All right, I'll stop fussing. You won't mind if I worry a little while you're gone, will you?" She gave him another gentle hug then went on. "So, what do you plan to do about Ronni?"

"Do about Ronni?" He gazed at her with wide eyes, color rising in his face.

"Igor, it's easy to see that you're besotted by the girl, or woman, I should say."

"Da, she makes me crazy, but I like it, and can't seem to stay away from her."

"She doesn't appear to mind," Ella replied, an indulgent grin playing across her lips.

"Yeah, but you said it yourself, woman, not girl. She is a woman and I'm still an unproven boy."

"Ah, so this mission is your chance to prove yourself as a man worthy of her attentions?"

"Da. I want to go anyway. I want to help, to use the things everybody has taught me. I want to show the king that the Children of the Wolf can be useful and valuable allies, not just helpless animals to protect."

"Oh, Igor, Harald doesn't see you that way, any of you."

"Perhaps, but as things are now we're little more than a burden to him. I want to change that, so he sees us as valuable assets."

"You've been training with Eric again, I see. I can hear his style in your words."

"Yeah, and Mr. Tommy. He calls me his sorcerer's apprentice. I like that and want to learn all he can teach, ..."

"But you're craving a bit more action? Ah, and you think Ronni will be more impressed with a man of action like Eric, more so than a man like Tommy. Igor, she's a smart cookie, I'm sure she can see the value in either man."

"Perhaps, but would a combination of both be so bad? It would make Igor unique among men, yes?" Igor said, as he straightened his shoulders and flexed his back.

Ella chuckled at that. "Oh, my young friend, you've got it bad. I can see some of your alpha drive at work here. Igor, Ronni is part hawk now, and hawks aren't pack animals, they can be fiercely independent. Are you sure about this?"

"I am, but I doubt she is. As you said before, she's a woman, and I'm little more than a child by human standards."

"Perhaps, but, we're not completely human, are we? I can see that your body has matured faster than a human's would, and I can also see that your thinking is changing to that of a man. I'll leave it to you two to work this out, but I caution you to ..."

"...think through every step and accept both the consequences and results of my actions?"

"So, you were listening to me after all," she quipped affectionately.

"Miss Ella, you're having way too much fun at my expense. Do I make such a fool of myself when Ronni is near?"

"Actually, I think the both of you are cute the way you flirt shamelessly with each other. And yes, I'm teasing you to make you blush. I'll stop now let you get ready."

"Da, leave the poor wolf some dignity to carry on his first important mission." She chuckled as she hugged him and lightly kissed his cheek before leaving the room.

BACK IN NEW YORK, OTHERS were making preparations for the same mission. "Director Compton?"

"Egan, I want you to monitor this operation closely. Keep a low profile, but get the goods on Sawchuk."

"Sir?"

"Look, we both know he's using foreign nationals on American soil. Why? What do they have on him? What has he already given away? What will he give away? What's their true objective? Have we already been compromised? The man's a complete wild card, and I want him in a place so dark he'll never see light again. Yes, we need him for this, but as soon as it's done I want to put him away forever.

"I should have finished him when I had the chance. I'll never understand why I didn't. I'm relying on you for this one, Egan."

"Yes, sir. I'll go pack and get on the road now." He left the director's office shaking his head. The director was letting this get personal, and when working with Sawchuk, that could only bring disaster.

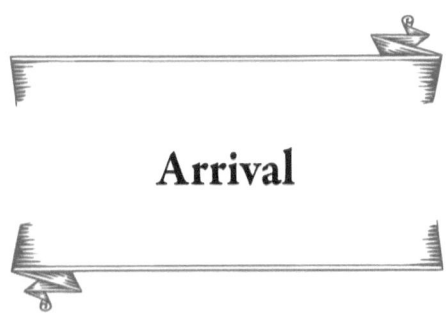

Arrival

The next morning found the team in the air for a short flight to Boone, North Carolina. While in flight, Clara brought the rest of the team up to speed on hers and Ronni's theory about what had happened, but she made no mention of the hawk's immortality.

Terry sat nodding his head. "Makes sense to me. What about you, blondie?"

Gudrun gave him a look that spoke volumes and he flinched away, grinning. "Yes, Agent Sawchuk," she replied tartly. "It does make sense at that." The twinkle in her eye took the sting out of her remark. "How do you want to handle this?"

"First I want Clara and Ronni to have a look and give that lab the once over. As soon as they report in, we can better judge what to do about the lab part of the mission. While they're doing that, the rest of us will make sure we're clear of prying eyes and ears, and then go on the hunt for the ones that got away. See if we can track them down."

"Excellent. What's our story on Ronni? They'll have a missing person's file on her that says they only ever found her clothes, not a single trace of the body," said Gudrun.

"What do you think, Kylie?" grinned Terry. "Secret recruiting job by our mysterious agency? We picked her up, she switched into uniform, then we made her disappear?"

Kylie grinned. "Yeah, I like that better than her being grabbed by white slavers."

"I don't," replied Gudrun. "Think about this for a moment."

21

Terry stopped and considered her feedback. "You're right, honey," he conceded. "The secret agency thing is too far-fetched. We can't be sloppy, Kylie. We need to sharpen up."

"Okay, give me a minute." Her fingers flew over her keyboard for a moment. "All right, this'll do. There was a gangland style shootout a few months ago down south. The police believe a bunch of slavers got wiped out by another gang. No arrests have been made.

"Ronni, you were taken by slavers and tossed into a van. The next day there was a lot of gunfire. Terry and a bunch of mercenaries killed your captors and rescued you. They recruited you to work for them and so you have been ever since. Will that work?"

"It's a bit out there," sighed Gudrun, "but I think it'll work. Now, how are we going to explain this plane to the authorities?"

"Don't plan to," replied Terry. He took out his phone and called ahead. "Egan? Yes, we're in the air. Look, I'm in an experimental plane and don't want to explain to the public ... okay, got it. Yes, we can, no problem. You'll bring the mobile lab there? Perfect."

He stood and moved forward to the cockpit. "Eric, here's our landing coordinates. Small government airstrip with a hangar for us."

"Sweet." Eric tapped in the information into his console. "Got it." Terry patted his shoulder then returned to the others.

The plane landed easily and taxied into the hangar. A man who'd been waiting outside with a van stepped inside and lowered the doors. He called out as he approached the people descending from the plane. "Terry, good to see you. This all your people?"

"Hey, Egan, it's been a long time. Yeah, this is the advance team. They'll look the situation over, and if necessary I'll call in a cleanup crew or whatever we might need to get it done."

The man nodded. "Your mobile lab's right outside. I've booked a half dozen rooms at a hotel near the lab. I'll drive you in, then pick up my car from there and lead you to the scene."

"Sounds good, Egan. Got some stuff for me?"

The man grinned as he passed Terry a briefcase. "Your badges and other supporting documents are in there. Pick up your hotel keys at the desk. The director says if you want a rental car too, you can pay for it yourself."

"He's still pissed at me, isn't he?"

"You quit before he could fire you, then took your whole crew of experts with you. Wouldn't you be pissed?"

"Yeah, guess I would at that." grinned Terry.

The man suddenly looked at Ronni suspiciously. "Wait, I think I know that woman's face. She's on the missing person's list. Shit, she knows exactly what happened in that lab."

He moved past Terry and toward Ronni, but stopped short as Igor and Gudrun stepped in his path, shoulder to shoulder. "Sawchuk, what the hell?"

"Relax, Egan. If you've got questions for Dr. Stockman, ask, but be polite."

"What, or the kid and the woman will beat me up?"

"Try me," said Gudrun. Something in her voice caught his attention and he made eye contact. Suddenly he recognized something about her. Swallowing hard, he took a step back.

Ronni spoke up then. "You want to know what happened to me and where I've been. I'll tell you. I was checking out a hawk caught in a power line when two rednecks grabbed me. I woke up in a motel room, naked. I was sold to another man who took me away. The next day there was a lot of gunfire and these people killed my keepers, they found me and brought me out.

"They said they needed a researcher; I've been working for them ever since. I have no idea at all what happened in my old lab."

"That's the worst bullshit story I've heard in years, but I guess it'll do. I don't even want to know the rest, but why the kid, what does he do?"

"The kid?" asked Igor, giving him a hard look. "What kid?"

"You. You sound like a Russian to me."

"I used to be one," replied Igor, his voice going hard and his stance shifting.

"So, what's your job with this team?"

"That's classified."

"Sure it is, kid."

Terry saw Igor's jaw twitch. "Igor's our tracker, Egan. He grew up in the forests of eastern Russia. If you ever get lost in the woods, this is the guy you want looking for you. Now, stop trying to interrogate my team, or we'll have to make you disappear. Let's get this show on the road."

The man led them outside and everybody climbed aboard the big van for a short ride to the hotel. Terry checked them in and then arranged for a rental car, an SUV with off road capabilities. By the time they arrived at the lab, Egan was getting nervous. Gudrun's eyes followed his every move.

Gudrun leaned over and spoke softly to Terry. "This man could become a problem."

"He's Compton's right-hand man. Probably got orders to observe, record, and watch for a good excuse to make me disappear forever. Keep an eye on him, sweetheart."

"With extreme pleasure, lover. Can I intimidate him a bit?"

"Go for it, enjoy yourself."

Gudrun smiled wickedly.

Clara and Rhonda got out of the van in hazmat suits and headed for the door. Gudrun followed but stopped beside Egan. They watched in silence as the two women slid open the lab door and entered, closing the door behind them. As the door closed, the man swallowed hard and spoke. "I know who you are."

"Oh?" she replied, arching an eyebrow at him. "And just who is that?"

"You're Gudrun Arielsdottir, born in Iceland, trained in several countries of Europe. You inherited an elite team of mercenaries from your mother who then disappeared, you're unbelievably successful at infiltration and assassination. You work out of Germany for the most part, but you've been in America for the past two or three years, or maybe more, but nobody knows how you come and go, or why."

"I'll tell you why," she replied. Her voice was so cold he shivered and stepped back. "I come to spend time with my husband, Terry Sawchuk, and I'll be extremely unhappy should anything ever happen to him. Do you understand me?"

He gulped and stepped back further. "Yes, I understand."

"Good." She turned her attention to the two women working inside. They were gathering samples of the dust as well as the blood and tissue scattered around. Egan slunk away and stood near Terry.

"So, you're married to the Angel of Death are you?"

"Is that what they call her?" Terry grinned. It was surprisingly amusing to see a trained agent shaken, even if only for a moment, by the love of his life.

"That's what she's called in mercenary circles, only takes the really hard jobs, never fails, swift, deadly, unstoppable. They say she's the one who took out Stephan Krebs, international super crime boss, among others."

"Yep, that's my girl. Word to the wise, never call her blondie, or goldie. It makes her cranky."

"Good advice."

"Egan, I know why you're hanging around, and I'll be straight with you. If Compton comes at me, she'll take him out. Anybody else in the way will just be collateral damage. You know how she works, a surgical strike out of the blue, in and gone, no survivors. And this time it would be personal for her." Terry shifted and faced Egan.

"Look, we'll do you good on this, the whole thing will be explained away, the missing people will be dealt with, and the green shit will be disposed of. We've seen the results of this stuff before. Believe me, you don't want a bunch of government lab geeks messing with it. Bad things can happen when it gets into the wrong hands."

Egan's eyes widened, "You know what it is, don't you, Terry?"

"Yeah, I do. Egan, you and I both know our government is run by a bunch of paranoid morons, so was the old Soviet Union. This crap is one of their fuck-ups. Everybody wants to make super soldiers the easy way. This, what happened here, is the result of that kind of thinking.

"Take a look at that blonde goddess over there, trained from early childhood, familiar with all manner of weapons, electronic surveillance, and a master of battle tactics as well as hand-to-hand combat. That's how you make a super soldier, not with crap like this," said Terry, pointing toward the lab.

"Go back to the hotel, Egan. Have a few drinks, kick back, and relax. I'll bring you everything you need, all nice and neat."

"Yeah, you're right, Terry. Hell, I don't even want to know the truth." With that he walked back to his car and drove away.

Igor poked his head out of the mobile lab. "He gone?"

Terry nodded, then grinned as the young man took a device from his backpack and began to inspect the vehicle. A few minutes later he returned to Terry, holding out his hand to show his prizes, three listening devices and two tracking units. At the boss's nod, he set them on the ground then stomped them with his boot, rendering them useless.

Terry scratched his chin, speaking softly behind his hand. "There's probably a listening post in a nearby building."

Igor just grinned. "Mr. Tommy gave me the answer for that. It's already set up inside and working. All they'll be able to hear will be static."

Terry smiled as he gave the young man a friendly slap on the shoulder. "Igor, you're hired."

Gudrun returned to him then. "So, he left? Did I overdo it?"

"No, my darling, you didn't. I'm sure Compton was listening, so I added a bit of my own. I said that, should anything happen to me, you'd go after Compton."

She smiled and rested her forehead on his. "You weren't wrong there, my lover. So, Igor, are we clear?"

"I believe so, Miss Gudrun."

"Take another look around, just in case." He nodded and began a new scan of the vehicle, inside and out. He found nothing. "So, what else did you tell him? What's our story?"

"I told him the green shit is old Soviet Union attempts to create super soldiers."

"Okay, so that's our story?"

"Yep, Kylie's making up the paperwork on it now. It's old Soviet stuff, got lost in the world when the wall came crashing down, and pops up occasionally to create havoc. That's our story. Once Clara and Ronni clear the lab, we'll clean it up, make it all shiny, then close the government case."

"But we'll still be working on it, right?"

"Yes, my love, we'll stay on it until we're certain it's clear. I'm not telling King Harald it's done until I'm dead sure it's well and truly done. I want to fully account for each and every human being who was adversely affected by this accident."

WHILE TERRY AND HIS team waited for the lab to be cleared, Director Compton grew increasingly frustrated. He arose from his desk and paced about the office. Nothing. Not a goddamned thing on Sawchuk's whereabouts or activities over the last two years. Why? Why was the man being so secretive? What was he hiding? How the hell was he hiding it?

Compton sat back down and placed a call. He was bloody well going to find out what Sawchuk had been up to. When the three agents arrived, the secretary showed them in.

"Director Compton, you've got something special for us?"

"I do, Hayes. You're going to North Carolina with me. I'm fed up with this crap."

"Sir, isn't Deputy Bridger already in Boone, sir?"

"He is, but he and Sawchuk were partners once. I think he might be a bit soft on the guy. No, we're going and we're going to get the goods on Sawchuk. You know what they say, if you want something done right, do it yourself."

The Hunt Begins

Clara and Rhonda came out of the lab and Terry locked it down while they changed out of the hazmat suits and secured their samples. Once that was done they returned to the hotel where Igor swept the rooms for listening devices. He found and destroyed several. They then gathered in Terry's room for a brainstorming session.

"We all clear, Igor?"

"We are now, Mr. Terry. I found three bugs in each room. I need to check the rooms every time we return, or each time the housekeeping staff come through, yes?"

"Yes," replied Terry. "Sadly, we're working for a group of people who don't trust us. They think we'll hide important information from them. They'll play every dirty trick in the book to get that intel from us, and the truth about us. We have to figure this out, deal with the situation, and keep any and all information about us or the incident out of government hands."

"So, it's business as usual," grinned Kylie."

"Business as usual, Kylie. Clara, what's your assessment so far, and what's your next move?"

"A good meal and a few hours in the lab. It's too early to tell much of anything else yet," she replied. "You got anything, Ronni?"

"Some. I checked the time sheets and made notes. I have a good idea who was in the lab when it happened. I recognized two of them and managed to keep my stomach down. We've got at least eight people unaccounted for."

"So, what aren't you telling us?" asked Clyde. Ronni nodded. She'd come to recognize that Clyde was the best profiler and psychologist in the business. He hid a sharp mind and keen insights behind that mild-mannered, geek look. She sighed and let her shoulders sag. "I saw pieces of three very dangerous animals in that lab."

"So, somewhere out there are at least three people partially changed into these animals, if they managed to survive this long?" asked Terry. She just nodded. "So, what could we be dealing with here?"

"Grizzly bear, mountain lion, and crocodile for certain, maybe more. Things were often shipped to this lab from all over the country."

"Oh? Why?"

"Making sure it was safe for the students to work with them," she sighed. "I have no idea if any students were there or not. They often came in late and forgot to sign in."

"Well, crap. Kylie ..."

"Already working on it, Boss. Missing person's list coming right up. Here's the official one, but I'm checking for students who went missing about that same time."

"Awesome as always," grinned Terry. "Ronni can work on that with you, unless Clara needs her in the lab."

"Actually, I do need her in the lab, Boss. Two sets of eyes will be helpful on this one."

"Okay, once Kylie has a list she can show it to Ronni, see if anything clicks. Now, on to the nosy government. Clyde, talk to me."

"All right, Terry, here's how I see it, but it's pretty wide open right now. Compton's still pissed that you quit before he could fire you. He always resented you for some reason. That was easy to see when we all worked for him."

"We have history," grinned Terry.

"I'll just bet," replied Clyde, matching his grin. "The thing is, I'm not sure what his endgame is, or if he'll get frustrated and start upping the ante. He already knows you've used foreign mercs on American soil.

Now he knows you have access to some high-end technology, like the plane. He'll reason it out that the plane is how Gudrun's team can come and go undetected."

"Shit, we blew that. Now he'll start looking hard at the new Lair. When he can't see that area from satellite he'll get serious and start probing. He could even come in heavy."

"I'll deal with this," said Gudrun as she rose to her feet.

"Goody, what are you going to do?" asked Terry.

"Tell you later, honey, right now I have to go hunting. You can bring me up to speed when I get back." Gudrun swept up the keys to the rental car and walked out of the room.

Terry and Kylie exchanged looks then went back to the brainstorming session.

EGAN BRIDGER SWALLOWED another gulp of whiskey and sighed. He still hadn't made his report to the Director. This was one report he truly didn't want to make. As soon as Compton learned that the Angel of Death was married to Terry Sawchuk he'd want full twenty-four-seven surveillance on them, and it would fall to Egan to get it done. He'd looked into her eyes and saw his own death there. No, he was in no hurry to make that call, for he knew he'd be the first casualty when she went after Compton.

Suddenly there was a knock on the door of his hotel room. It startled him and he involuntarily jerked, spilling his whiskey. "What?"

"Room service, personal delivery," came a soft feminine voice.

"Just leave it outside."

"*Open this door, now.*" That wasn't a human voice, but a voice of command from some distant hell he could not imagine. Obediently he rose and went to the door, unable to stop himself. His eyes flew wide in terror as he saw Gudrun standing there.

She put a hand on his chest and thrust him back into the room then stepped inside and closed the door.

"What do you want?"

"Tell me the truth, what did you report to your superiors about us?"

"Everything."

"Did you mention the experimental plane?"

"No, only that you flew in."

"Did you tell them who I am?"

"No."

"Why are you spying on us?"

"Following orders."

"Why were those orders given?"

"Sawchuk's a wild card. He has access to unknown and superior technology as well as secret information about anomalies within our borders. He's holding out on us and endangering the country. We don't really know who he's working for or what his goals are."

"Listen carefully. Terry Sawchuk is the only man standing between this country and certain doom at the hands of outside forces. He must be protected at all cost. You must help him in every way you can. Do not trust Director Compton, he's working against Terry, against the good of the country. Compton is weak, he cannot be trusted. Only Terry Sawchuk can be trusted. Do you understand?"

"I understand. I'll do everything I can to help Terry and stall Compton."

"Go to sleep now and forget I was here. When you awaken, you will remember what I have told you and know it is the absolute truth. You will know what you have to do."

"Wake up and remember to help Sawchuk," he muttered, as he laid down on the bed. He was completely unaware of her leaving the room.

Terry looked up and grinned as Gudrun returned to the room. "So, how was the hunting?"

"Just fine, dear."

"Is Egan Bridger still alive?"

"He is, and now he is also an ally. Compton is still unaware of the plane, and he will remain so. In future Mr. Bridger will be a valuable resource to us."

"Had a chat with him, did you, Gudrun?" Eric asked, already knowing the answer.

"I did, Eric, yes. He was an obstacle, and intimidation wasn't quite enough to ensure his cooperation."

Eric grinned at Terry. "Told you."

"Gudrun, you're amazing," said Terry. "I don't know what I'd do without you."

"You'll never have to find out, my lover," she replied with a twinkle in her eye.

Terry chuckled and went on. "Okay, Gudrun's dealt with that, so what's our next move? Options? Opinions?"

"I think Igor and I should do some scouting," said Eric. "Who knows, we could get lucky."

Igor stood up. *"Finally!"* he thought to himself. One thing he wasn't good at was sitting on the sidelines. His alpha instincts rebelled every time he tried.

"Okay, you guys do that, and I'll go poke around the streets, check in with the local law enforcement, cruise the bars, etc. See what I can shake loose."

"Actually," said Gudrun, "Clyde and I can check the bars while you do your detective thing."

"All right," Terry conceded, wondering what his wife had in mind. "Clyde, try to keep her out of trouble."

"Me? Clyde's the one who'll bear watching. You know what these quiet types are like."

Terry laughed and rose from the chair. "All right, people, we have our assignments. Let's see what we can come up with. Meet back here in six hours." He kissed Gudrun's cheek and walked out.

Igor was delighted to be assigned to work with Eric. The man was a well experienced mercenary, a wealth of information and useful skills, and he was willing to teach the younger man. More, Eric always treated Igor as an equal, a brother-in-arms. They took a taxi back to the lab, then started walking around the block. "Mr. Eric, do we have a plan for this?"

"Just Eric, Igor, we're comrades-in-arms now. Yes, we do have a plan. I wondered if perhaps some of the escaped people might be hanging around this area, trying to get back into the lab. You know, return to the scene, find a cure for what's happened to them. I can watch for people trying not to be noticed. You my friend, have another task."

"I do?"

"Yes. Jimmy told me how you scented or sensed our quarry before. You can tell if you detect something different, unnatural, right?"

"Da, that I can do. So, we're a team, you're the eyes and I'm the nose and ears, yes?"

"Exactly," said Eric, giving the young man a friendly clap on the shoulder. He watched as Igor, seeming to just be looking around, cocked his head slightly to scan the air for scent and sound.

They continued to widen their circle, taking their time. It was about an hour later that Igor caught the scent. "Eric."

"Where?"

"Behind us, I think. It was just there and then gone."

"We'll circle back." They picked up the pace slightly, turned the corner, and headed back. They were about three blocks from the lab. As they turned the next corner he caught the scent again. "Again, I smell it, woman and not woman, mouse and not mouse. She is near."

"Slow down now, Igor. Tell me if the scent is getting weaker or ... there she is. Don't look at her, she'll sense your eyes. Across the street, beside the blue car. If we can ... dammit, she spotted us. She's leaving. I didn't get the license plate number, did you?"

"Da, and her picture. See?" Igor showed Eric his phone.

"Good job, little brother. Good job. So, she had her hair and most of her face concealed, yet what skin we could see was very pale."

"Disguise, do you think?"

"Yes, I'm sure that's a disguise. You sensed the wrongness in her, yet she drove away so she is still functional. We have the plate number, so Kylie can track her down. I'm thinking it'll be better if Ronni makes contact first."

"Because they will know each other?"

"Yes. The woman should trust Ronni, and through her we can learn much of what has happened here. Igor my friend, we got lucky."

"So, it's still early, we should keep looking, yeah?"

"We should keep looking. The more intel we gather, the better for our leaders to make a plan that'll succeed." They continued their scouting until it was time to return. Igor sensed one more, but the scent was days old, and they saw nothing.

WHILE ERIC AND IGOR continued their scouting mission, a badly shaken woman drove back to her hideout, her grandfather's cabin in the hills. "That was too close," she muttered to herself, her deformed hand shaking on the steering wheel. "Far too close. That man spotted me. But it was the young one with him that scared me the most. There was just something about him, something feral, hungry, dangerous.

"He moved like a predator. That's it, he moved like a predator, and he sensed me. They're looking for me. They probably know I survived the accident and want to take me to some hidden lab to experiment on me. No way in hell that's going to happen."

"OKAY FOLKS, WE'RE ALL here, said Terry as he closed the door to his hotel room. "Report. Kylie?"

"I've got that missing person's list whittled down, Boss. Ronni can look it over and see if she recognizes anyone who wasn't on the official checked-in list."

"Awesome. Clara?"

"We performed a number of tests, Terry. It all points to our original theory. The powder is inert now, and I'm thinking they must have had a small chunk of actual meteorite to set it all off. The lab can be cleaned up now.

"On the identifying side, we've isolated eleven different sets of DNA, but there's only enough actual body mass in that lab to account for four bodies. Everybody else got away."

"Okay, great so far. Gudrun, how did you and Clyde make out?" She just smiled sweetly. "Clyde?"

"We hit several bars, Gudrun got propositioned a dozen times, groped a few times, broke three sets of fingers, I got slightly drunk, and we learned nothing of value."

"Bummer," grinned Terry. "Eric?"

"Igor and I scouted around a bit and got lucky. Igor scented something not quite right, what was that again, Igor?"

"Woman and not woman, mouse and not mouse, very fearful."

"Yes, that was it," Eric went on. "We spotted her getting into a car. Igor got a video of her."

"I can show you on Miss Kylie's computer," grinned Igor as he connected the phone. In a moment, they saw the short video. Igor froze the image with a clear view of the license plate.

Kylie grinned as she wrote it down. "Igor, my man, you rock! I'll have an address for you in a minute."

"There's no need, she won't be there," said Ronni.

"Talk to me, Dr. Stockman."

"Her name is Justine Henley, Terry. She has an apartment in the same building as mine, but she wouldn't try to hide there, it's too vulnerable. Two years she inherited a small cabin up on the ridge. She'd go there when she wanted to be alone. I'll bet that's where she is."

"Did you know her well?" asked Gudrun. "Do you think she'll trust you if you approach her?"

"I knew her well enough. We weren't close friends or anything, but we worked well together. Under normal circumstances I'd say yes, but I'll be reappearing after vanishing months ago, and who knows what this event has done to her mind."

"Clyde?"

"Well, she can still drive a car and find her way around. I'd say her mind is still pretty much intact, but she's been traumatized, probably terrified, and obviously hiding some sort of disfigurement. If a mouse is her avatar, her first instinct will be to run and hide."

Terry nodded. "Eric, did she spot you?"

"Yes. I'd say her prey instincts are pretty sharp."

"Dammit. I truly hope she doesn't bolt."

"Probably won't," said Clyde. "She doesn't know either of these guys and doesn't know Ronni's with them. She'll run back to her safe place and hide there for a while, waiting for the danger to pass."

Terry rose and began pacing as he absorbed this information. At length he stopped and sat back down. "Ronni, can you find this cabin of hers?"

"Yes. I've never been in it, but I picked her up once when her car broke down."

"All right, we need to know what she knows. Gudrun, this is your kind of action. Take Ronni, Eric, Igor, and Clyde. Get Ronni and Clyde close enough to talk to her without scaring her to death."

"Understood. What are the goals, our objectives?"

"We need Ronni to gain her trust, learn as much as you can about what happened, where the survivors might be hiding, and who they are. Goody, don't let anyone see any of you, if they do, make sure they have a memory lapse." She nodded her agreement.

"Ronni," Terry went on, "if she's functional, convince her to go to the Lair for sanctuary. Eric, you arrange transport for her. Igor, you find out if there are any others with her."

Rhonda saw the look between Terry and Gudrun. "What was that? I saw the look you gave her, Terry. What did that mean?"

To their surprise, it was Igor who stepped in. He rose and stepped close to Ronni, reaching to take her hands in his and looking into her eyes. "Sweet Ronni, you know we must not leave her running loose to be discovered by others. We will not kill her, she's not dangerous, just afraid. If we have to we will restrain her and take her back to the Lair."

"And lock her away for the rest of her life?"

"Perhaps at first, for her own safety, and to keep her secret from the public, but she can function, she can reason. We will find a way to help her once we have gained her trust, just as we did with you."

Rhonda nodded, sighed, and squeezed his hands tightly for a moment then he stepped away. "Just don't scare her to death. The hawk has a strong heart, but I doubt a mouse could survive your style of therapy."

"His therapy? What did I miss?" asked Clyde.

Eric grinned and winked at Ronni who blushed and threw a cushion at him. "Shut up, Eric."

"You were doing interviews, Clyde," smiled Gudrun. "Ella and Torvil were trying to help Ronni master the change, but she just couldn't make it work. Suddenly a wolf leaped at her and snapped its jaws close to her leg. Ronni flew up to the rafters then back down and started beating Igor with her wings. A moment later she changed back and commanded him to stop laughing and put his pants back on."

"It was the same for me as a pup," said Igor, grinning at Ronni. "Owan scared the crap out of me, and I changed and ran away. It took them two days to track me down. Sometimes a person needs some help for the first few times. Besides, she got me back."

That made Ronni laugh. "Oh yeah, I got you back, right, Clara?"

"Up until that point I had no idea a wolf would fit under a sofa," grinned Clara.

"Ladies please," moaned Igor, "leave the wolf some dignity."

Rhonda reached out to ruffle his hair. "No way, buddy. He was in the great lounge, showing off for one of the Lair's housekeeping staff. I dropped down from the rafters and grabbed his tail. He just about turned himself inside out.

"Igor, I still haven't thanked you properly for all that. Our game of scaring each other made it possible for me to master the change, and to get comfortable with it. I owe you, my furry friend." He just smiled shyly and blushed. "Just don't do it to the mouse, she'll die of a heart attack."

Igor was still looking at Ronni as his gaze turned cool and his heart sank. He felt the flush on his face deepen. "She still sees me as a child!" As he gave words to the thought, he felt a surge of despair. "I have to find a way to show her what I can become, what I am."

Ronni thought she saw hurt on Igor's face. Regardless, the man looking at her now was a far cry from the teen she'd pranked. She suddenly regretted sharing that piece of history the way she did. She opened her mouth to say something to him, but he had turned his gaze away.

"All right, people," said Terry. "You folks do what you do, Kylie and I'll stay here and keep Egan out of Clara's hair while she works. Get some rest, folks."

Trapped Mouse

It was just after midnight when they set out. Ronni struggled a bit as she drove, searching her memories for the right turns. It took hours, but finally, she stopped on a dusty dirt road. "Okay, I remember now. There are three cabins just ahead. Justine's is the last one in the row. Most likely the others will be empty now, they're mostly used for weekend getaways."

Gudrun took over, she'd do this like a mercenary strike. "Igor, you, Eric, and I will make certain the area is clear. If you find anyone else nearby, signal me and I'll deal with it. Ronni, as soon as we have the area cleared, and the cabin surrounded so she can't escape, we'll signal you. You and Clyde go in, drive right up to the door, making enough noise to alert her. Be careful, I doubt she's dangerous, but best to be safe."

The three camo clad figures vanished around the bend in the road as dawn lightened the sky. The young werewolf slipped through the trees to the first cabin while the two mercs moved on to the second. He soon joined them. "All clear," whispered Igor. "I scent nothing new. No human has been there in many days."

Gudrun winked and patted his shoulder. "This one is clear as well. Eric, you and Igor circle the cabin, check to make sure she's there."

"She is," said Igor. "Her scent is fresh and I can hear her stirring."

"Is she alone?" asked Gudrun.

"Yes, she is alone. I sense no others near."

"Nor do I. Eric, check anyway, then take up a sniper post." He nodded to Gudrun and trotted off. Catching the look Igor gave her, she relented. "We dare not take any chances."

"So, no matter how certain the thing is, you prepare for the worst anyway?"

"Yes."

"Miss Gudrun, thank you for taking the time to explain this to me, but you are team leader, you need not explain."

"We have the time, my young friend, and you can't learn if no one will teach you. I'll watch the front, Eric is setting up by that tree. You circle around the back and prevent any escape from that angle." He nodded and vanished around the building, as silent as a hunting wolf. Gudrun sent the text for Rhonda and Clyde to approach.

There was a sudden sense of panic as the big SUV pulled up near the cabin door. Inside the woman remained as still as death, barely breathing, desperately trying to still her pounding heart. A knock came at the door, but there was no sound from inside.

"Justine, it's Rhonda Stockman, remember me? Justine, I know what's happened to you. I'm here to help, please let me in." Still no sound came from within the cabin.

"Justine, it's all right, I'm not here to hurt you, I'm here to help. Look, the same thing happened to me. I'm not here to take you in to be studied or hurt, I'm here to help you. Justine, please talk to me." Still only silence.

"Okay, I know you're scared to death, I was too. Justine, I'm coming in. I have a man with me. Clyde's a friend, you can trust him." So saying she tested the door, but it was locked. Gudrun suddenly appeared at her side, and with a single twist, broke the lock. She then slipped back out of sight.

Rhonda pushed the door open just a crack and suddenly heard scurrying inside, as though someone was trying to escape. She stepped through the door, but the open window told the tale of the woman's departure.

Suddenly they heard a series of high-pitched screams from outside. Gudrun appeared around the building at alarming speed, but there was no need, the wolf had caught the mouse.

The terrified woman screamed and squirmed, but she was held fast in strong arms. Slowly she ceased her struggles as the soft voice began to penetrate her awareness. "Hush now, beautiful lady, hush. Igor's got you. I won't let anyone hurt you, my little mouse. Be still now, be still. Igor will protect you."

She stilled in his arms, but he continued to soothe her with his voice and the power she sensed in him. This was a predator of terrible power, but he was being so gentle. It was the young man from the day before. His full attention was focused on her. At that moment, there was no one else in the world but them, no threat, no fear. Slowly her terror subsided, and she melted into his arms.

"Hush now, my little mouse. You are Justine, yes? I'm Igor. I will protect you. We'll take you to a safe place where the world can't get to you. There are others like us there. You will be safe and happy there, you'll see. Trust Igor now."

Wide fearful brown eyes searched his for any sign of betrayal but found only gentle compassion there. Finally, she nodded and melted back into his arms. "Can you speak?" he asked. She shook her head no. "Perhaps with a computer, yes?"

Slowly she disentangled herself from his arms and showed him her disfigured hands. One was almost completely a mouse paw, but the other looked as though it might function. Tears suddenly flowed from her eyes as she lowered the scarf from her face to show a half mouse muzzle. She let him look then moved the scarf back.

With a look of compassion and understanding he took her in his arms again. "Da, Igor understands, he does, little mouse. It's hard for you to eat and you're hungry, frightened. You don't know who to trust.

Let me show you." Gently he turned her towards Gudrun. "I told you there are others like us. Watch now.

"Miss Gudrun, would you please show Miss Justine your tiger?"

Gudrun instantly understood. If he showed her the wolf or if Ronni showed her the hawk, it would frighten her again, but to see the half tiger would help her to understand there were others who couldn't fully transform. She nodded, then slowly changed into full vampire mode, being careful to make no threatening moves.

The woman in Igor's arms moved deeper into his embrace, whimpering, her eyes wide as she gazed at the half tigress before her. Slowly it began to penetrate her terrified mind, this creature meant her no harm. These people were like her, they had somehow gained control of it and could return to their human form.

She turned back to gaze into Igor's eyes again. "You see, little mouse, there are others like us, like you. We'll take you to a safe place, we will help you. Will you trust Igor to keep you safe?" Again, she searched his eyes then slowly nodded. "Thank you. Will you help us to understand what happened to you and the others?" She nodded slowly.

"Miss Gudrun, Ronni is needed to help Clara. Perhaps you folks could go report in to Mister Terry. I'll stay here to protect Justine. I think if Kylie and her computer came, Justine could tell us much."

"I like it, Igor. I'll leave Eric with you just in case. Do you need Clyde too?"

"Actually," said Clyde, "I think the fewer people here, the safer she'll feel, and the easier it'll be for her to relax. Leave Igor here with her and Eric outside, then we should go back and report in. While you're doing that I'll contact the king and arrange for a welcome at the Lair for Justine."

Gudrun nodded, spoke to Eric, then they climbed aboard the SUV and drove away. Igor was still holding Justine in his arms. "Come on, let's go back inside where no one can see us, yeah? Come." Gently he took her deformed hand in his and led her back inside. "Eric, Justine needs food that's easy to eat, do we have anything with us?" He then closed the door.

A moment later there was a sound outside the door. She startled, but he held her gently. "It's okay, little mouse, it's okay. That was Eric with food for you. I'll just get it; you stay right here. She didn't though, she clung to his hand as he opened the door and pulled the backpack inside. He popped the top off a liquid meal replacement, but she just shrugged her shoulders.

"Right, you need a straw. There should be ... ah, here they are." He pulled the wrapper off the straw and put it in the drink then held it steady while she drank it all. He opened another and she finished that as well.

"Feeling better?" She nodded. "Good. Now, we have time to wait, so I'll tell you about the Lair, the safe place. Come. Sit with me and I'll tell you a story. Come." He sat on the old couch, and she shyly came to curl up beside him. He could tell by the way she moved and sat that there were problems with the rest of her body as well.

Igor put his arm around her thin shoulders protectively. "The Lair is like a big castle, too many rooms to count. We even have a king and queen. There are many people like me, some like Miss Gudrun, one werebear, one werehawk, a writer, several humans, and some others in between. All live and work together.

"So, before we came here, the king told us to help the people who were injured as much as we can. The Lair will be a much safer place for you, and once we finish here, Miss Ronni and Miss Clara will be able to help you."

She looked puzzled, so he went on. "Miss Clara is a genius. She and Miss Ronni work together in the lab to learn as much about us as they can. You could call them our doctors. They're here with us now, but they'll return to the Lair. Mr. Terry will probably want to send you there as soon as possible. If he does, I'll ask to go with you. My sister,

Nikka is there too, and I'll ask her to be your protector until I can return."

Her big eyes searched his for a moment then she nodded. She snuggled onto his shoulder once more and sighed. "Ah, your belly is full now and your body wants to sleep. We have time, little mouse. You nap and I'll hold you safe." She sighed again then closed her eyes. For the first time in weeks she felt safe, safe to sleep.

Debriefing the Mouse

Justine awakened with a start when the car returned and a door slammed. She squeaked and huddled deeper into Igor's embrace. "Hush now. Easy, little mouse. Igor's got you. There's nothing to fear, it's just Miss Gudrun returning with our people. Be brave now. I promise no one will hurt you. Okay?"

She swallowed fearfully then nodded. "Come in slowly," he called. The door opened and she flinched as a powerfully built man came in, followed by several others.

"Perhaps we're frightening her," said the smaller man, as he adjusted his glasses.

"You are," replied Igor, "but our Justine is a brave woman. She knows you won't harm her. Justine knows that, even as I'm her protector, so are all of you. Look, little mouse, there's Eric who brought you food and guarded the door. There is Miss Gudrun who's just like you. You've met Mr. Clyde already, and this man is Mr. Terry. He's our team leader and Miss Gudrun's mate.

"This woman is Dr. Ronni, you know her from before. You're friends, yeah? And this woman is Miss Kylie. She's brought her computer so you can talk to us."

"I'll set it up here on the table," said Kylie. "There, all ready to go." She slipped out of the chair and stood aside, giving Justine plenty of room to approach.

Igor stood and helped Justine to her feet. "Come, my brave mouse, let's give this a try. I'll stay right beside you. Would you like that?"

46

She nodded and, gripping his hand tightly, went to the table and sat to the computer. She stared at the blank page for a long moment then brought her deformed hands out of her sleeves. Slowly, carefully, she tapped a few keys with a claw. "Igor, thank you."

He smiled and kissed the top of her head. "You're welcome, Miss Justine. Mr. Terry will ask you questions now. I'll stay right here for you, and read out your answers so everyone can hear. Mr. Tommy taught me to read English so I could work computers with him."

She looked up at Igor first, then at Terry and nodded. He began. "Ma'am, we truly do need your help here to understand what happened in the lab. First off, are you Justine Henley?"

She nodded yes, so he went on. "Are you the only survivor?" She shook her head no. "Do you know where to find the others?" Again, no.

Terry nodded. "Okay, we believe that, after Dr. Stockman disappeared, some of the green residue from her accident was brought to the lab for study. Is that correct?" She nodded yes. "Were there any suspicious stones brought with it?"

She turned to the computer and tapped carefully. "Only one," said Igor.

"Okay, this will be tougher. Please take your time. Tell us what happened as best you can."

She sighed and began to tap on the keys. Twice she stopped, frustrated, but tried again. Suddenly Igor's eyes opened wide. She had begun to pick up speed and her hands were changing back to normal.

Her powerful need to share her experience, her all-consuming desire, caused her hands to revert to their original form. Her fingers fairly flew across the keyboard as she typed. Everyone held their breath until she stopped suddenly, gazing at her hands. She began to cry as they returned to deformed paws.

Igor swept her into his arms. "That was amazing, little mouse. Justine, do you know what you've done? Do you know what this means?"

She stopped weeping and gave him a puzzled look. "It means that you can learn to control the change. It was the same for Ronni. She couldn't change back until the need was too great for the spell to hold her. She has learned to control the change, and you can too. It'll take time and work, beautiful lady, but you'll be able to return to us one day. This is such wonderful news."

As the realization of what he'd said penetrated her anguished mind she gave him a bone cracking hug. She would be able to reverse the changes, she could become whole again. She sat back to the computer and began to write, a look of fierce concentration in her eyes. Once again, her hands changed and words poured out onto the screen. When she finished, she sighed and sat back, her hands reverting to paws.

Igor looked at the screen for a moment then began to read. "They brought the dust, stone, and Ronni's clothes into the lab on a Wednesday morning, two days after she'd disappeared. The search parties hadn't been able to find any trace of her or a body. Nobody even thought about wearing hazmat suits as the dust wasn't radioactive. It was months before anyone got around to investigating it all.

"John Ainsley was just lifting the stone from the box when he dropped it. It exploded into green dust, covering everybody and everything in the lab.

"I was farthest away from the blast, so I wasn't as deformed as many of the others. Some of them were so grotesque that it was impossible to believe. One of them, John himself I think, was part mountain lion, part black bear, and something else. He started killing people in his mad rush to escape.

"The way was blocked, but the fire escape door had been blown open, so I went out that way. I made it to my car and drove home. I realized what had happened to me and knew I couldn't try to enter the building in the state I was in, so I came here and waited for darkness.

"When night fell, I returned to my apartment and dressed to try and hide my deformity. I tried to get back into the lab, hoping to find a way to reverse this, but the police were there. I watched from a distance, and saw a number of other creatures like me, watching from the alley, and the rooftops. One was peeking out from the sewers.

"When the police left, we tried to get back inside, but it was locked tight, and our keys didn't work anymore. We left then, but I kept going back, hoping against hope that someone would leave it unlocked. As the days passed I realized the condition was getting worse. I was no longer able to feed myself without hands or a working mouth.

"I fell into despair, and began to ponder ways to kill myself. That's when you people showed up. It's becoming more difficult to hold my mind intact, to think straight, as the condition progresses. I believe that the others changed into parts of different animals, but I only absorbed the mouse I was holding in my hands at the time. It was terribly frightened, and I was trying to sooth it. It appears I've absorbed that fear as well.

"What is to become of me?"

"She stopped there for a moment," said Igor, before picking up where he left off.

"This handsome young predator with the Russian accent has somehow pierced the wall of terror that is trying to take over my mind. He makes me feel safe, and now, has assured me that, one day, I'll be able to control this and return to myself.

"He said you'll help me, provide me with a place of safety and help me. I'm afraid to trust, to dare to believe, but I can see my own hands now, and at last I have hope.

"She stopped there," said Igor. "Perhaps someone has another of those meal replacements for her?"

"Right here, brother," smiled Eric. "Last one. Need a straw?"

Igor nodded so Eric passed him one. Igor held the drink for her while she finished it all and sighed with relief. She looked up at him with worship in her eyes. Igor kissed the top of her head again then spoke. "Ready for more questions now?" She nodded so he nodded to Terry.

"This is a list of people we believe might have been in the lab at the time of the incident," said Terry as he passed it to Igor. "Can you confirm or add anyone to this list?"

Igor held it up for her to read, but Kylie spoke up. "That document is on the computer. May I?" Justine nodded then cuddled back against Igor as Kylie leaned across her to change the document. "There, does that help?"

Justine nodded as she studied the list. Without her realizing it her hands changed back as she reached for the keyboard. Igor grinned as he watched her work. Beside each name she wrote a single word - dead, escaped, or absent. She then added two names. One was a field supervisor who hadn't bothered to sign in, and the other was a student who'd arrived late. Igor read out the list for them.

"Well, that about covers it," said Terry. "Now, I expect you have some questions for us. Ask away."

Justine began to type, Igor reading her words aloud as she worked. "Igor has spoken of a place of sanctuary, of safety. I'm afraid to hope, but so very desperate at the same time. He spoke of a castle with a king and queen, it's so hard to believe. Can this tale possibly be true?"

Terry just grinned. "Oh yes, it's all true. In fact, I'm a bit surprised the queen ..." His phone buzzed. "Ah, that's her now. Hi Sally, you checking up on us again?"

The woman's voice was filled with mirth as she spoke. "Terry, I have to keep an eye on you, don't I? Put me on speaker and let me talk to Justine." He grinned as he put it on speaker and passed it to Igor who put it on the table beside the computer.

"Justine can't speak, Queen Sally," said Igor, "but the phone is right beside her. She can type her answers into the computer, and I'll read them out to you."

"Thank you, Igor." The woman's voice was filled with compassion now, and Justine allowed hope to rise within her. "Justine, you've gained a powerful ally and protector in Igor. He's young in years, but old in wisdom, experience, and fierce in his devotion to those he chooses to love and protect. Igor has promised you sanctuary and protection, the king and I will honor that promise.

"Come to us and we'll keep you safe, provide for all your needs, and there are people here who can help you learn control of the change. We also have people who can help you adjust, help you create a new life full of wonder. Please say you'll come, young Nikka is dying to meet you."

Justine's fingers flew and Igor grinned. "Who is Nikka?"

"Nikka is my younger sister," said Igor. "You must not let them meet, Queen Sally, Nikka will tell her all my terrible secrets. I will have no dignity left at all by the time I return."

There was a round of chuckles at that. "Too bad for you, Igor. Nikka's already informed us she will be Justine's protector in your absence."

Igor gave an elaborate groan and Justine actually made a squeaky laughing sound. She began typing again. "This is all too much to hope for, to believe. If this is all true, then I'll come if you'll have me."

"I'll ask the house staff to make up a room for you. What will you need?"

Justine didn't answer, she just looked at Igor for help. "She will need loose clothing, for her body is struggling with the changes right now," he said. "She will also need help with food as her jaws are causing difficulty. Nikka can help with that. I think also, our Justine might like a smaller, more cozy room, at least for a start, and a laptop computer so she can talk."

"Bring her to us, Igor. We'll have everything ready and waiting when you arrive. Justine, I can't wait to meet you." With that the queen was gone.

Ronni had been watching the way Igor hovered protectively over Justine, providing a sense of safety for the terrified woman. There was a maturity in her young friend that had escaped her notice, and she liked it. She had a new respect for Igor, and this deepened her infatuation with him, but now it was time for her to join him in helping the terrified girl.

Ronni stepped closer then sat on the floor at Justine's feet. "Justine, Clara and I have been working on this. I know you're struggling right now. Here's what I think is happening for you. You only blended with a single animal, and because of that, I believe you may be the only person from that day who will ultimately survive.

"You say the condition is still progressing. I believe that, once you're in sanctuary, you should release yourself to it, but only with supervision. There are people there who can help you with this. Once you've fully changed to your animal, you'll be able to change back fully. I say this because this is how it was for me. Watch and don't be scared."

Ronni pulled off her t-shirt and suddenly changed into the hawk. Justine squeaked in terror and shrank into Igor's arms. Ronni gave it a moment then changed back and dressed herself again. "You see, right now you're caught in the middle of the change, neither fully mouse or woman, but, as with your hands, when your need is greatest, that's when you can change.

"I've come to know Nikka, Igor's sister. You'll love her, but she can be impulsive. Igor, you need to show Justine what she's in for, or Nikka could scare her to death."

Igor nodded slowly, then gently pulled Rhonda closer and transferred Justine to her arms. "You cuddle with Ronni now, beautiful lady. Igor has something to show you. Don't be frightened, Igor will never harm you. Watch now, and know that Nikka is just like me."

He quickly shed his clothes then shimmered into the wolf. The dire wolf was huge and terrifying. Justine shrieked in fear and nearly fainted as Ronni hugged her close. "It's all right, Justine, it's all right. It's just Igor, your protector. The queen told you he was fierce and protective, this is why." Even as she spoke the wolf gave a soft whimper and dropped to a submissive posture at Justine's feet. He nuzzled gently at her foot then rolled on his back.

"See, watch now," chuckled Ronni. "He wants you to rub his belly. Like this." She reached down and began to rub the wolf's belly, and he groaned with delight. Tentatively, Justine also reached down to lightly rub the offered belly with her paw. This brought further groans of pleasure and a wag of the tail. Justine gave a happy little squeak then rubbed even more.

"All right, knock it off, Igor, and don't forget your pants this time," chuckled Terry. "Eric, you, Clyde, and Igor head back to the plane and take Justine to the Lair. Once you have her settled in, get back here as fast as you can. Oh, and bring another werewolf with you, Georg perhaps."

"You want more werewolves?" asked Gudrun.

"It was Igor's sense of smell that helped us find Justine."

"You're right, my husband, the wolves have a much stronger sense of smell than I do. We'll need them to track down the others."

The Search Goes On

The plane was in the air and a terrified Justine cowered in Igor's arms the whole journey. Meanwhile, back at ground zero, the team was back into the mobile lab. "Clara, what's the good word?"

"Nearly finished, Terry. We've cleaned up all the green dust, suspended it in water, and flushed it down the sewers. It's safe, it's completely harmless now, less environmental damage than the soap from washing your car. We've also gathered all the DNA samples and fingerprints we can. I say we let it go."

"All right, as soon as Eric gets back we'll grab the flame throwers from the plane and melt this bugger down. Egan can keep the fire department entertained until we get it done. Let's get back to the hotel for some rest now. I'll talk to Egan, give him a story for Compton, then we can start planning the next phase of the mission."

"And that is?" asked Rhonda.

"Ronni, you know what we have to do here," replied Terry.

"Just so there's no confusion, spell it out for me. I want to be completely clear about this." Ronni braced herself for what she knew was coming.

Gudrun rose and faced her. "You know what has to be done." Rhonda's eyes spoke volumes and Gudrun looked away. "This is why I hate working with amateurs. Look, we have to find those people, or whatever they've become now. If we can help them we will, but you said it yourself. Justine is likely going to be the only one who will survive."

54

Gudrun sighed as she turned back and saw indignation settling in across Ronni's features.

"So this is how it works," she went on relentlessly. "We locate, assess, then aid, or eliminate. Either way, there must be no trace of them ever found."

"I resent that amateur remark, Gudrun," said Ronni. "I'm a veterinarian, I know damn well some animals have to be put down, and I've done my share of that. I just wanted to be sure of what and how we plan to go about this. I'm well aware that it's unlikely we'll find another we can save, but I don't want any of them ending up as lab rats in some secret government compound either."

Terry watched the two women face off and swallowed hard. This could get ugly in a hurry. He sighed with relief as he caught the twinkle in Gudrun's eye.

"So you have the heart of the hawk after all," she grinned. "I apologize, Ronni. You're right, their end, if it must come, will be as swift and painless as we can make it. I also agree they must not end up in the hands of the government. I promise you; we won't let that happen. If by some mischance they've already captured one, we'll dig it out and remove it. Is that acceptable to you?"

Rhonda searched Gudrun's eyes for a moment then sighed. "Accepted. How can I help?"

"What can you tell us about any of the people on that list?" asked Terry.

"Well, Boone is a fairly small city, most folks lived outside of town. This fellow here, Jordy Banks, he was a field inspector, lived well out on a small hobby farm. If he could function at all, or if he could manage his thought processes, he'd probably head for home, they all would."

"I have a full list of the addresses matched to the names," said Kylie. "So, do we wait for the wolves to arrive, or do we get started?"

"We get started," said Ronni. "Many of the animals in that lab were nocturnal so these creatures will be more active at night."

"She's right," agreed Gudrun. "We should begin the hunt. Eric can catch up when he returns."

Terry sighed and rose to his feet. "And so to work. I have to talk to Egan, Kylie still has work to do on our cover story, and Clara needs to get some rest. Gudrun, looks like it's your hunt."

"I need Clyde for a getaway driver and Ronni for surveillance. She can give me a bird's eye view of the situation."

Rhonda turned to see the twinkle in Gudrun's eye. "Was that a catty remark?" Gudrun laughed and the ice between them was broken.

Clyde reached for the keys to the SUV. "Looks like I'm driving for Tweety and Sylvester. Let's go girls." He stopped as they were both giving him the look. "What, the human doesn't get to joke?"

"Clyde, don't make me bite you."

"Let him go, Gudrun, I'll poop on him from above. He'll never see it coming."

"As the official getaway driver for this hunting team, it will be my task to stay behind the wheel and be ready at all times."

"That or wear a hat," grinned Kylie.

Gudrun took Clyde's arm and steered him toward the door. "Come on, sugar, we've got work to do."

It was late when they arrived at the farm, but there was a full moon to give them light. As they got out of the car they became serious. Rhonda spoke first. "Gudrun, you know how this is done. How do I help you?"

"We change," replied Gudrun, as she morphed into the half tiger and strapped on her weapons, a stunner, a tranquilizer pistol, and a nine-millimeter side arm. "I'll start circling the farm from here, moving to my right. You fly overhead and see if you can see anything."

"I'll wheel to the right," replied Ronni. "If I see anything I'll call, then wheel to the left above it."

"Perfect. Good hunting," replied Gudrun. She set out, testing the air for unusual scents, Rhonda took two strides and leaped into the air, her clothes settling slowly to the ground.

A few beats of powerful wings and she was high overhead, slowly wheeling to the right as she searched the ground below for any large animals. Her sharp eyes saw them all through the foliage, mice, raccoons, deer, etc., and Gudrun. The vampire moved effortlessly and silently through the forest, a ghost from a nightmare of which the people sleeping soundly nearby were unaware.

About an hour later Gudrun heard the piercing cry of the hunting hawk. She looked up to see a small dark shape circling to its left just ahead and to her right. She moved silently in that direction. The creature was sleeping beside a deadfall.

What she saw made her pause. The beast had the head and right arm of a bear, complete with long deadly claws, but the left arm was slender, ending in a small hoof. The torso was partly human as was one leg, the other leg looked like it might be from a raccoon or some such animal. The tail curled around its body was thick and hairless.

As stealthy as she was, the creature sensed Gudrun's approach and leaped up with a scream of primal rage. Before she could get a weapon focused on it, the creature struck knocking her back and stunning her slightly. It attacked again, but the hawk dropped from the sky and raked its face. It batted the bird aside then took three shots to the chest. Puzzled it looked down, then took another step towards Gudrun. This time she put two in its head.

Rhonda lay where she'd fallen, watching the beast slowly morph back into a human male as it sank toward the forest floor, dead. "Aw, Jordy, I'm sorry this happened to you."

"Are you injured?" asked Gudrun, as she helped Ronni to her feet.

"I'll have a few bruises I'm sure, but I'm okay. You?"

"I'm clear. Damn, that thing was fast and strong. Thanks for the save. I'll carry the body back to the car. If you go running around naked in the moonlight the locals will think that witches are on the loose again."

"Shut up, Gudrun," chuckled Rhonda. "That way; there's a wide ATV trail leading back near the car. I'll meet you on the path with a body bag."

She leaped into the air and silently rose into the sky. The vampire slung the body over her shoulder and started out. She found the ATV trail easily. She hadn't gone far when Ronni met her with the bag. They put the body inside, then Gudrun carried it the rest of the way to the car which was now waiting at the trail's edge.

Gudrun placed her burden in the back of the vehicle then climbed into the back seat. "Is there a crematorium in this town?"

"There is," replied Rhonda. "We may have to break in, but ..."

"We will, Ronni. Clyde can double talk anyone who comes to investigate, and I'll put the compulsion on them as well. So, what's bugging you? I had to ..."

"I know, you had no choice. It's just the way it reverted to human as it died that shook me. Is there any way we can return the ashes to the families?"

"We'll need a story to jive with what we're telling the government, but, yes, I think we can do that. I'll talk to Terry about it."

"Thanks. I know this is a peace offering for me, and I do appreciate it."

"It's all right, Ronni, I understand. I lost my conscience the day I was made vampire, but I remember what it was like at first.

"Besides, I think your idea has merit on another level. If we return the ashes, then the families have no further reason to search for these people. These folks were in a bad lab accident, carried off to a secret hospital for treatment, but they didn't make it. The bodies had to be cremated because of the infection. Something like that should work and give their families some peace."

"And that will give me some peace," sighed Rhonda.

"Ronni?"

"I'm all right, Clyde, I am."

"You're not either. This was your first action, and I'm quite sure your first time to see a human body like that. This will affect you, and you need to be aware of it." Clyde's voice was full of concern for his teammate.

"And that's why Terry brought you along. It wasn't for the victims, it was because there were two newbies on the team. You came for Igor and me."

"The girl's pretty sharp, right, Clyde?"

"Indeed she is, Gudrun. Indeed she is. I believe you'll be just fine, Ronni. I'm just along for the ride."

"Bullshit, Clyde, but thanks anyway. Turn left there and it's that building up ahead. Lights are still on, somebody's working the night shift."

In the end, Gudrun had to put the compulsion on the attendant to make him comply. Under that spell, he was more than happy to help them. It was dawn when they left with a small urn of ashes.

While Kylie went to pick up Eric and Igor, and the night hunters got some well-deserved rest, Terry and Egan paid a visit to the victim's family, told their story, and returned the ashes. They found Eric with Igor and Georg waiting for them when they got back to the hotel. They took Kylie's list of addresses and set out for the more urban sites, but they found nothing.

Another Hunt

Next morning, the team gathered in a private dining room in the hotel for breakfast. Terry had arranged it the evening before, knowing the team had a tough night ahead of them. The group was surprisingly chatty considering how little sleep they'd all gotten. The room had been swept for bugs but there hadn't really been a need. Conversation this morning was focused on each other as opposed to the mission. It was moments like this that reminded Terry of why he was so proud to be part of this team.

Igor was enjoying his omelet when Rhonda sat down on the chair next to him. She poured herself some juice and quietly spoke.

"I didn't get a chance to tell you what a wonderful thing you did for Justine. It wasn't just what you did, but how you did it. You made her feel safe because you inspired her trust and confidence."

Igor had stopped eating and was now gazing at her. "You let her draw on your strength, Igor, and find her own courage." Rhonda swallowed as she lost herself in his dark eyes. She felt her own color rising.

"Thank you, sweet Ronni," he said without smiling. "I remember what it felt like to be scared like that. No one should have to feel scared and alone, especially after such a trauma, after having her whole life stripped away like that. I gave her what is mine to give, my friendship and my loyalty." Igor's eye's softened as he added, "Everyone needs family, a hawk, a wolf, even a mouse."

60

A warmth washed over her as she sat next to the dire wolf, listening to his voice speak of loyalty and family. Rhonda nodded and smiled back at Igor, turning her focus to her food. Oh yeah, pack animal all the way. She liked that about him.

After breakfast Terry convened the team in the mobile lab to confer.

"We were called in late on this situation, and people are suffering because of it. We need to get moving. Clara, you stay with the mobile lab, Eric, Kylie, Georg, you're with me. First, we burn the lab to destroy any evidence we might have missed, then we take another shot at the urban sites. Gudrun, you take the others and check out the next rural address on the list. Let's roll."

RONNI WAS DRIVING AS they headed out of town. "You're being awfully quiet, Igor. Missing your girlfriend already?" she teased.

"My girlfriend?"

"Justine."

"Ah, my poor little mouse. She's so frightened, Ronni. You should see the room they made for her. It's quite small, no windows, very cozy. I think she'll learn control of the change in time, and then she won't be so frightened. It's the mouse's fear she feels most. When she defeats that she will master the change easily just as you did, my pretty bird," Igor teased back.

"You were exceptionally gentle with her, Igor," said Clyde, "almost overly protective. What was it about her that triggered that response in you?"

Igor smiled wistfully before he spoke. "She was so much like Nikka, my sister. When first we were taken by Stephan Krebs' men, Nikka was the youngest and frightened more than the rest of us. They would shout at us to attack the training dummies, but they frightened Nikka so, she just cowered behind me.

"One day a guard struck her with a pain stick when she refused to attack. Several times he touched her to make her scream. Marco, Krebs' second in command, stopped him and said to throw her to the dogs. Anyone who wouldn't obey was thrown into a pit of hungry fighting dogs. The man grabbed Nikka by the scruff and walked towards the dog pit. I attacked him.

"They activated the pain collar on my neck, but it just drove me on. I ripped him open and got Nikka behind me, away from the men. Marco stopped them from shooting me. He said I could keep Nikka alive as long as I remained so savage, so I agreed.

"Miss Justine's cries of fear were like Nikka's, terror beyond reason. I couldn't help myself."

"That may have been it at first," grinned Rhonda, "but are you sure that's all of it?"

"Well, okay, she cuddles nice, what more can I say?" They all chuckled at that, but Ronni had a strange look in her eyes and there wasn't a lot of sincerity in her laugh.

At that point they arrived, it was another small farm. They stopped to look the place over for a moment, and as they did a man ran from the house and jumped in a truck. He headed right for them, pulling up beside the SUV so he could talk with the window down. "You folks might want to make yourselves scarce," he said. "Stay in your car and just drive away."

"Normally, I'd take that as a threat," said Clyde. He'd rolled down his window to talk to the man.

"It's not a threat, mister, it's a warning. There's a chupacabra running loose.

"What the hell's a chupacabra?"

"It's a monster. They're rare as chicken's teeth, thank god, but every now and then one appears. This one showed up a while ago and started killing everything in sight. It's killed horses, pigs, cattle, and I think it got my wife's brother. He went to work one day and was never seen again. We were out of town for a few days and when we got back he was gone, just vanished.

"I went out to hunt the damn thing two days ago, but it got in the house while I was gone. I got back to find my wife and kids up in the hay loft and a dead cow on the barn floor. I called the wildlife people and left a message, but they never got back to me.

"Look, it ain't healthy around here. You should move on for your own safety."

"Yes, well, that's why we're here," replied Clyde, as he showed his badge. "We're here to remove the threat."

"You know what that thing is, don't you?"

"Yes, my friend, we do. Look, do you folks have a safe place to go for a few days? Give me your cell number and I'll call you when it's clear for you to return home." The man gave him the number and Clyde wrote it down. "All right now, you go back and gather your family. We'll stand guard until you're clear. Lock your house up tight then head out, we'll find and neutralize the threat."

The man nodded then turned his truck around and drove back to the house. They followed and waited outside. A short while later a group of people came out, looking all around nervously, and piled into an old car then drove away.

"Clyde, that was masterfully done," said Gudrun. "All right people, I'd say we're in the right neighborhood. Igor, you go left and I'll go right. Ronni, you circle to the right to search, then left if you spot anything."

Rhonda nodded then leaped into the sky. Igor watched her for a moment then gathered her clothes and passed them to Clyde. "Are you going wolf?"

"Da, I'm stronger as the wolf," he replied, shedding his clothes. With that, he morphed into the dire wolf and leaped away towards the nearby forest. Gudrun passed his clothes to Clyde, then shifted into full vampire mode and followed.

Clyde sighed and leaned back against the SUV. "I sure hope nobody shoots one of them for a chupacabra."

Clyde didn't know how close he was to the truth. Rhonda, flying high overhead, saw the man just as he spotted the wolf. The hunter raised his rifle, but before he could pull the trigger a hawk's cry rent the air and something struck his weapon. "What the fucking hell...?"

He grabbed up the fallen weapon then approached the hawk which lay stunned on the ground. His eyes opened wide in shock and disbelief as it morphed into a naked woman holding her head and groaning. "Just what in god's name are you?" he asked as he leveled the rifle at her.

She had no time to answer as something hit him from the side. Powerful jaws clamped down on his shoulder and he was ripped off his feet. The gun fired once as it was torn from his hands and sent flying, the bullet going harmlessly into the ground. Whimpering in terror, he faced the huge snarling wolf. With bared fangs, it advanced on him.

The woman surged to her feet and grabbed the wolf. "No, don't. Don't kill him." The huge beast turned to nuzzle into her, sniffing her and licking at her face. "Stop it," she said, as she tried and failed to fend off the friendly assault. "I'm all right. I am, honest, I'm fine." With that reassurance, the wolf turned back to the hunter. He'd recovered his rifle and was bringing it to bear.

The shot went wild as the wolf took him again. The woman begged him to stop, and he backed away, leaving the man on the ground, bleeding. Suddenly the wolf shimmered into a young man. He grabbed the rifle and hurled it away into the trees. A fist bunched in the man's shirt and he was hauled to his feet by a powerful arm. "I think she's hungry," snarled the boy as he thrust the hunter away.

Turning to see what the youngster was looking at, he screamed again and tried to run. The vampire had him in a heartbeat, sharp fangs biting deeply into his neck. He struggled weakly then relaxed and melted towards the ground.

The nightmare thrust him away and turned to the others. "We'll discuss this later. Lady Hawk, are you harmed?"

"I'm fine."

"Wolf?"

For an answer he morphed back into the huge beast and shook himself. "Very well then, resume the hunt." She turned to the man cowering on the ground. Whimpering he crawled away. At least he tried. She caught him by the collar and hauled him back to his feet.

"What were you doing here?"

That voice from a distant hell demanded an answer. Trembling in fear, he struggled to find his voice. "Hunting the chupacabra," he squeaked out.

"Why did you try to kill the hawk and wolf?"

"There's a bounty on wolves. I tried to shoot it but the hawk attacked me. I thought it was hurt so I tried to shoot it, but it changed into a woman then the wolf bit me."

She snarled as thought she might kill him, and he wet himself. *"Listen carefully. You saw the chupacabra. It was covered in fur, body like a bear and the head of a lion. You panicked and ran, losing your rifle as you fled. You saw nothing else, just the chupacabra. It bit you, but you got away. Now go!"*

Gudrun watched him go then resumed the hunt. She remained in vampire mode while they slowly circled the farm twice, they found nothing. It was growing dark as they returned to Clyde and the car.

Clyde heard the cry of the hawk and held up her clothes as she made a swift landing. She was pulling them on as the wolf raced from the trees and leaped into the back seat, morphed into Igor, and began getting dressed. Gudrun was close behind them, back in human form. "I found only a scent and tracks, you?" she asked.

"The same," replied Igor.

"I got nothing," said Rhonda.

"Clyde, take us back to town, these two need to eat."

"What about you?"

"I've been fed already." He said nothing more as they closed the doors and he drove away.

Back at the hotel they reported to Terry. As she finished her report, Gudrun turned to Rhonda. "Tell me what happened back there."

Rhonda sighed and began her story. "I was watching for movement, any movement. I saw that hunter aim at Igor, so I screamed a warning and dove at him. I tried to grab the rifle barrel, but he flailed with it and knocked me down. I was winded and hurt. I changed back to try and get some breath back into my body. He pointed the rifle at me, and Igor took him down."

"I thought the wolf would kill him."

"Why didn't you, Igor?" demanded Gudrun.

"I would have," he replied, "but Miss Ronni asked me not to. I wanted to kill him, but..." He shook his head and looked away.

"That was a mistake," said Gudrun, as she took him by the shoulders and looked him in the eye. "The man was a coward and a fool. He saw a naked and hurt woman, yet he pointed a rifle at her. A vampire would have a hard time explaining a dead body that had been drained of blood, but a wolf kill would be no problem.

"I saw you turn your back on a wounded enemy, Igor. That's a bad mistake."

Igor nodded, as he knew Gudrun was right.

Gudrun continued to gaze into his eyes for a moment then relented. "All right, lover boy, but swear to me, never again."

He smiled in spite of himself and nodded. "I promise."

She released him and turned to Rhonda, her eyes ablaze. "What the hell's the matter with you? Were you trying to get him killed?"

"Hey, back off, sister." Rhonda was on her feet and nose to nose with Gudrun.

"Be silent and listen."

Rhonda's mouth worked, but no sound came out. She swallowed hard, and nobody else in the room moved a muscle. Vampires didn't use the compulsion on friends or allies.

"Now that I have your full attention," said Gudrun, "I'll explain a few facts to you that'll help keep both you and your teammates alive in future. Ronni, I'm not your enemy here, I'm a friend, and a fellow non-human.

"This is the main point you have to get through your head, you're not human anymore. As you saw today, the humans will fear you because they don't understand you, what you are. They'll kill anything they don't understand. That man tried to kill Igor, he tried to kill you, and he might have succeeded if Igor hadn't been as fast as he is.

"Ronni, you have to let go of those old reactions, that old training. You're a member of a team now. When on a mission the object is to accomplish that mission with all hands remaining alive. It doesn't always happen that way, but we have to try. Today you let old reactions take control and nearly got both of you killed." She gazed into Rhonda's eyes for a long moment then spoke a single word. "Release."

Rubbing her throat, Rhonda glared at Gudrun. "Don't ever do that again."

"I won't," sighed Gudrun. "Ever. Just promise to help me keep the team alive, and I swear I'll never do that to you again."

Rhonda nodded and lowered her gaze. She knew Gudrun was right. She could have gotten Igor killed today.

"Who was he, Miss Ronni?" asked Igor.

"I have no idea, Igor."

"Not the man today, my pretty bird, the other one." Igor reached out and lightly touched her hand.

"Other one? What other one do you mean?" Rhonda pulled her hand away and folded her arms across her chest.

"A long time ago, some man told you many lies. He told you to be weak. He told you that men should never be harmed, even if they hurt you, even if they attacked you. Who was he?"

She stared at the young man with the compassionate eyes. Her face registered anger, defiance, and then deep sorrow. "My father," she replied. "I'm so sorry to put you in danger, Igor. I could've got you killed. I'd just die if anything happened to you, but I couldn't stop myself. I guess that lesson was burned into my psyche pretty deep."

"Igor, you'd be a natural at my line of work," said Clyde.

The young man smiled shyly, then rose and took Rhonda into a gentle hug. "It's all right, Lady Hawk. Igor was watching with his ears. I wouldn't let him harm you again. Miss Gudrun is right, though. We must let go of our past and protect our pack. It's easier for the wolf, we understand the idea of pack by our very nature. The hawk hunts alone, it's harder for you."

"I guess you're right," she said, as she returned the hug, then kissed his cheek and stepped out of his arms. "Gudrun, I'm sorry. Help me, teach me... oh, you just did, didn't you?"

"There's defiance behind that sarcasm. Your resistance to me is old, an authority issue."

"Yeah, that would be me, old issues-with-authority Ronni. I'll work on it, Gudrun, I promise I will."

Gudrun smiled and held out her hand. "Accepted. Still friends?"

"Yeah, I guess," replied Rhonda, as she grasped Gudrun's hand. "You know, I think we went about this all wrong today."

"Oh? Care to enlighten us?" said Gudrun.

"Look, I know I'm the newbie here, but it seems to me we went wrong from the start. You went full vampire and Igor went wolf. Yes, your senses are keener that way, and you're stronger, faster too."

"But?"

"But a human with a gun will shoot either one of you on sight. However, the sight of another human with a gun wouldn't arouse the same fear. Even in human form, your senses are keener, stronger than most. The way Igor found Justine proves that."

"I believe you're right," said Gudrun. "I just don't want that damned creature to jump me when I'm not at full power. All right, next time Igor and I'll work together in human form, carrying artillery, and you scout from above. Don't try to help us, just be our eye in the sky."

RHONDA WAS SHARING a room with Clara. As they settled down for the night Clara spoke. "Let it go, girlfriend. Gudrun is who she is."

"I know, and she's the best in the world at what she does. I just wish she'd cut me some slack, you know? I'm no mercenary soldier."

"No, you're not, and you should stop trying to be one. You're the hawk lady. Soldiers work in units, wolves run in packs, but the hawk hunts alone. She answers to no one, she makes her own decisions, answers her own call. You're trying to be one of Gudrun's troops and it isn't working for you, it goes against your nature. Now, tell me about the rest of it."

"Rest of it?"

"You've got the hots for Igor, right?"

Rhonda blushed deeply. "Shit, am I that easy to read?"

"Yeah, you don't hide it all that well."

"He knows, right? I feel like such an old cradle robber. Shit, are they going to throw me out of the Lair?"

"No fear of that," chuckled Clara, "and speaking of wolves, they mature early and are truly loving creatures. Speaking from experience, I can see the attraction."

"You and Georg?"

"Yep."

"What happened?"

"He wants a hundred pups, I don't. We're talking about it."

"Aw, sweetie."

"Stop trying to get me off topic. The Igor thing is for you guys to figure out. The Gudrun thing is different. You need to talk to her, not with your hackles up, but as equals sharing a common goal."

"Yeah, you're right. Thanks honey."

"G'night Ronni."

Rhonda drifted off to sleep with thoughts of Igor. He'd been so loving and gentle with Justine. *"Damn me for an old cradle robber, but I'd give anything for him to hold me like that."*

IN ANOTHER HOTEL, A man was getting frustrated and letting it show.

"Director Compton, I'm sorry, but I've got nothing, and Egan's not saying anything either. I saw them go through that lab with flamethrowers before Egan gave you the all-clear on that issue. I have no idea what they destroyed or what they're doing about the missing people."

"Goddammit, Sawchuk must have gotten something on Egan. I know that bastard's using foreign nationals on American soil, and I intend to put a stop to it. Starting tomorrow, Grady, you and I have work to do, we'll get started first thing in the morning. I want to be in place before they sit down to breakfast. I'll tail Sawchuk myself."

With that Director Compton shut off the phone and sighed. "Dammit, Sawchuk, I have no idea what you're up to, but you're not getting away with it. I'll let you clean this up, but I won't let you dispose of all the evidence, no way in hell. When you're finished, I'll haul your ass in for a proper grilling. You'll be lucky if you or your pet mercs ever see sunlight again."

The Hunt Goes On

The next morning the hunters set out again. Igor drove while Gudrun and Rhonda sat in silence. When they arrived at the farm he stopped and hopped out. "Talk to each other, ladies." With that he scooped up his weapons and trotted off towards the trees.

"Is he okay with those guns?" asked Ronni.

"Eric's been teaching him; I wouldn't give them to him if I wasn't comfortable with..."

"Whoa, whoa, Gudrun, that wasn't a criticism, just me being a worrywart. I didn't mean ..."

"I know you didn't," said Gudrun, allowing her shoulders to relax. "Your boyfriend is right, though, we do need to talk."

Rhonda blushed crimson. "Dammit, Gudrun, don't you start too."

"Sorry."

"The hell you are," replied Rhonda. "I can't help it. I know it's all wrong, but ..."

"He gets your motor running?"

"Oh yeah, big time. What's up with that? Like, why the hell does he turn my crank like this?"

"Ronni, I'm so sorry, I should have seen more clearly yesterday. Igor's right, we do need to talk. I know all too well what's going on with you, and I should be doing the big sister thing, instead of the drill sergeant thing."

"Gudrun?"

"Let me tell what I think's happening for you. When I was first made vampire, I clung to Ella like a kitten to its mother, but all too soon we grew apart. You see, my emotions were maturing at the same rate as the tiger that had become a part of me. I left and was a solitary hunter for many years.

"Now, I think your hawk is getting broody. Is it nesting time for them now?"

"It's a bit late, but yeah, it is. Holy shit. Do you think...?"

"Oh yeah, I surely do, girlfriend," Gudrun grinned wickedly. "I'd say your hawk is a teenager, horny as hell, utterly defiant, and ready for independence. I came on like big mamma authority figure, and your feathers came right up."

"Well crap, so now what do I do?"

"Talk to somebody and listen, Clyde maybe, or Amanda, when we get back. They were a big help to me when we were all forced into tight quarters."

"Yeah, Clara said something else about this."

"Oh?"

"Yeah. She pointed out the hawk is fiercely independent, not a natural pack animal. Add to that my natural authority issues, and you've got one messed up bag of feathers on your hands. She said I'm trying to fit myself into your troops, but it's not a natural for me. I'd be a shitty soldier."

"Don't like taking orders?"

"Nope. Sorry."

"All right, so how about this, you're not one of my troops, you're an independent scout. You gather information, relay it to me, and my people deal with it from there."

"Gudrun, you'd be okay with that?"

"I stayed awake all last night trying to figure out a way for us to work together efficiently. I believe this is it. So, little sister, time for us to get to work. Find me that beast."

Rhonda grinned, then leaped into the air with a piercing cry. Gudrun watched for a moment the swept up her weapons, locked the vehicle, then set out on foot. This time she followed behind Igor. Two hours later she heard the hawk's call and looked up. The hawk was making a tight circle to the left.

Gudrun shifted to full vampire killing mode and set out at a dead run. She heard three shots ahead then the enraged challenge of an animal. She arrived to see the wolf, bloody and bleeding, standing over the dead body of a naked man. It looked as though it had been torn apart. It had.

As Gudrun arrived the hawk dropped from the sky, morphing into a naked woman just as she landed. Igor changed back as well.

"Igor, report."

"I found the beast, Miss Gudrun," he said, as Rhonda caught the first aid kit Gudrun tossed to her. He flinched once as she began to clean his wounds. "I had it in my sights, but it sensed me. It moved just as I pulled the trigger. I hit it, but not a killing wound. It charged at me and I fired again, but missed.

"It leaped on me, and I lost the rifle. It fired as it was torn from my hands. The beast was fast and strong, but no match for the wolf; I fought worse as a pup. I killed it, and it changed back to the man as it died."

"Ronni, report."

"I spotted it about the same time Igor did. I started my circle left then Igor shot at it. The rest happened too fast, there was nothing I could do." She patted Igor's cheek. "There you go, handsome, all patched up and good as new. When we get back I'll give you a shot of antibiotics just in case."

"You did right, Ronni," said Gudrun. "Your job was to find it. Our job was to kill it. This is how it works, girl. This one was a win. Now, here's the car keys, how about you fly back and bring us a body bag."

"Toss 'em up." Gudrun tossed the keys high into the air and the hawk grabbed them as she leaped toward the sky. She disappeared from sight with the keys dangling from her talons.

"Looks like your girlfriend's getting pretty comfortable in the air," grinned Gudrun.

Igor blushed and laughed. "Da, she's all hawk and wild as can be now."

"You like it."

"Far more than I should," he sighed.

"Igor?"

"Grandfather has forbidden this. All are directed to find human mates and to make many pups."

"But you'd rather run free with Lady Hawk."

"I can't help it, Gudrun. She looks at me and my belly turns to jelly, my knees shake, and I forget my own name."

"Oh little brother, you've got it bad. Come on, let's get going before she comes back and skins us alive for slacking." He laughed and slung the body over his shoulder as Gudrun led the way.

WHILE GUDRUN AND RHONDA were sorting themselves out, Terry had an unwelcome visitor. He and Georg were slowly circling the block while Eric lounged on a park bench, supposedly reading a book. It was just a flash of light, but it lit up all Terry's instincts. "Dirty rotten son of a bitch."

"Terry?"

"Huh? Oh, nothing, Georg. My mind wandered I guess."

The slight movement of his head from side to side told his companion there was a problem and not to speak. Georg glanced around, then sighed, his keen eyes had spotted it too. "I'm getting tired, think I'll take a load off and rest." He ambled over to share the bench with Eric.

"You do that," said Terry. "I'll head back and check on Clara."

As Terry walked away Georg sat on the opposite end of the bench from Eric. "Across the street, third floor," he said softly, as he bent to tie his shoe. Eric set his bookmark then stood and walked away.

Meanwhile Terry reached the mobile lab where he found Clyde, Kylie, and Clara. They looked up as he entered. "Kylie, we've got a code orange."

"What? Oh for the love of mercy. All right, I'm on it."

"I'll go check in with Egan."

So saying Terry left the lab and caught a taxi back to the hotel. He changed out of his suit and into sweats with a hoodie. He was soon back on the street.

Gudrun and crew returned soon after darkness fell. They found everybody else waiting for them in the mobile. The look in Terry's eyes said there was trouble. No one spoke as Clyde started the engine and drove away. As soon as they were outside of town Terry spoke. "Kylie?"

"The vehicle's clear, Boss."

"Eric, are we being followed?"

"Yes. Two different vehicles."

"Shit. Clyde?"

"There's no way in hell to shake them, Terry, not in this rig."

"All right, find us a look off point, anything with a long view and a parking lot."

"There's one just up ahead. Pulling in."

"Okay, everybody out and make like you're looking for something." With that Terry hopped out of the van just as the two cars drove by. The people in the cars all looked away as they passed, but Terry saw what he wanted to see. Only someone with something to hide would look away from a viewpoint.

"Kylie?"

"We're good. I've got Tommy's scattering device running. They won't be able to hear us."

"Clyde?"

"They knew we made them," he grinned. "They drove away."

"I make it five in all," said Terry. "Eric?"

"Yep, I count five. Georg?"

"Da, I saw five people."

"I count five," said Kylie. "Gudrun?"

"Five spies, yes, and I think I know one of them from somewhere. Terry, what's going on?"

"It was Compton. I spotted him this afternoon, and Egan confirmed it. Compton's in town. As near as Egan can figure it, and I do agree with his assessment, Compton's after my hide. He knows something's fishy, and he's still pissed that he didn't fire me and lock me away, he let me go. He doesn't know about the compulsion you put on him, but he knows letting me go was against the grain."

"So, what's his game now?" asked Gudrun.

"I'm only guessing, but past experience tells me he's planning to grab the evidence before we can destroy all of it. He probably wants to capture all of us, especially me, in the bargain. Egan says he hates the fact I've used foreign nationals inside American borders. Kylie?"

"Yep, that sounds about right. Compton's a raging paranoid. He thinks everybody in the world is out to sabotage the U.S. and he makes it his mission to stop them. We need to be careful here, people. If Compton gets his hands on any one of us he'll make us disappear forever."

Terry was swearing under his breath and the others fell silent waiting for him to speak. "Okay, this changes everything," he said at last. "Normally we'd just disappear in the night, but we can't do that. We have to play this out without getting locked away in the process. Here's what we do. We stay focused on point, but we mark the agents who're watching us.

"I hate looking over my shoulder all the time, but that's our only option. We have to finish this, and we can't kill the agents or Compton, as much as I'd like to. Here's the plan. We stay on point, but we have two objectives now.

"All non-humans stay in human form unless you're absolutely certain you won't be seen. People, we can't bluff our way through this one, these are trained agents. Kylie, I want a location for every damned one of those people. You locate them. Gudrun, you and Eric find and neutralize every damned listening and observation post they set up. They'll set up new ones as fast as you take them down, but it'll give the rest of us a chance to complete our mission.

"Ronni, I have a special task for you, if you're willing."

"Sure. What's on your mind, Terry?"

"We really need your eye in the sky, but people are watching. I need you to stay in hawk mode any time the public can see you."

"Excuse me?"

"Igor leaves the hotel with a hawk on his fist, and he returns the same way. By doing it this way you can still work from on high, but those watching us will have no idea what the hell is really going on."

"Sounds like fun," she grinned. "So, are we working in town or are we headed into the woods?"

"Woods. Georg and Eric both agree that there's no fresh scent left in town. Clyde and I will strap on the grungies and head into the sewers, see what we can scare up there. With luck, Compton himself will follow me in. He needs to get some dirt on his shoes.

"Okay, so you guys dealt with that one today? Got some ashes for me to deliver?"

"They're in the car, honey," smiled Gudrun. "He got the jump on Igor, but Iggy went all super wolf on him and he was dead by the time I got there."

Terry grinned and slapped Igor on the shoulder. "Good job, buddy. You okay?"

"I'm fine. Dr. Ronni patched me up and I'm good as new."

"Awesome. Look, you and Ronni will be the lone hunters now. Don't try to be a hero. Call for back up if you need to. Okay?"

"I will, boss. Promise."

"All right, folks. Let's get back to the hotel for some rest, tomorrow the job just gets harder."

WHILE TERRY AND HIS troops settled down for the night, Nikka found Justine staring at her hands, watching as they changed into paws and back again. "Hey, that's really good, you can control the change of your paws. Awesome."

Bright eyes met hers then Justine pointed to her legs. She changed them back to her human legs, but as she did her hands changed to paws. With a squeak of frustration her legs changed back and she slammed her fists on the small desk. She sighed and turned to the computer. "Another failure. I can change most body parts, but I can't hold more than one at a time. It's either hands or legs, but not both at the same time." She stopped typing and tears leaked down her cheeks.

"Oh sweet Justine, don't cry. Igor would not want you to cry. He would be proud of what you've accomplished. Rest now, rest, for tomorrow will bring new victories."

Justine returned to the keyboard. "I have to be able to do this, Nikka, I have to. When Igor gets back I want to show him a whole woman, not some mangled mutant mutt."

"Stop this now, sweet Justine, you must stop. Miss Amanda would say you must love the girl inside before she will come out. Here, I'll stay with you tonight. We'll work the other way."

"The other way?"

"Perhaps you won't be able to fully change back until you first change fully to the mouse."

"Nikka, what makes you think that?"

"Mr. Torvil. He thinks that might be the answer you seek. We could ask him about it in the morning." Justine sighed again and nodded. "Come, we will make a nest here for the night." Nikka fluffed up the straw that was on the floor to make it easier for Justine's deformed feet. She then shed her clothes and shimmered into the wolf. She turned to the right several times until she was satisfied, then she lay down and gazed up at Justine with big soulful eyes.

Justine reached out to scratch Nikka behind the ear then she allowed her hands to become paws again. She lowered herself to the floor and cuddled into the warm fur of the wolf and closed her eyes. The wolf nuzzled her affectionately, licked her face, then settled down, her eyes watching the door carefully. There was no danger here, but her protective instincts were aroused anyway.

Upstairs Sally relaxed back into Harald's arms. "She's sleeping now, and Nikka is in full watchful wolf mode."

"What do you think, sweetheart? Will she ever master the change?"

"She will, my love. I've seen her as a valuable member of our people. After all, a mouse can go where a wolf or a tiger can't."

"Now that's the truth of it," chuckled Harald, as he turned out the soft bedside light.

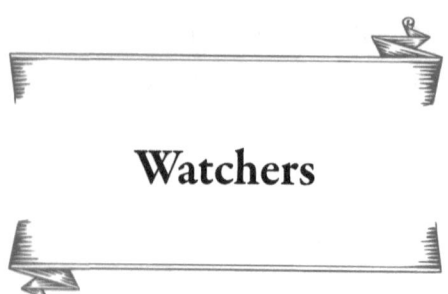

Watchers

The next morning, they gathered in Terry and Gudrun's room, preparing to set about the business once again. Kylie already had a location for all five agents, she had picture ID as well. "Kylie, you're amazing," grinned Terry. "Okay guys, memorize these faces, these people are now the enemy, but an enemy we dare not kill, rather, an enemy we must deceive. First thing we do is everybody rents their own car. That way we can scatter and drive them nuts.

"Ronni, you and Igor take the SUV, but wait until we've had a chance to engage the watchers." She nodded as he passed Igor the car keys.

They all rented a car, then drove back to the now burned out government lab. They got out, swapped cars, and then everybody went in a different direction. Terry grinned as he and Georg entered the sewers, a glance over his shoulder revealed a shadow following.

As the others left, Igor settled back to finish his coffee. "How are the wounds this morning?" asked Rhonda.

"Good as new," he replied, as he pulled off one of the bandages to show her a freshly healed arm. "See? Wolf heals fast. Wait here, Miss Ronni, I have to get something." He rose and left the room. Stepping out of the elevator, he entered the hotel gift shop, but soon returned with a pair of deerskin gloves.

"My pretty bird has talons," he grinned. "So, do we have an address to find, or do we just go hunting? It's a big forest and we have no idea where to look, or what to look for. How do you want to do this?"

Rhonda spread out a map of the city and surrounding area. "The lab is here," she said, tapping the map with her finger, "so most likely anything wild and frightened would go this way, shortest distance to the forest.

"Tell me, how does the wolf hunt for food?"

He gave her a slightly bemused look, thought for a moment, then spoke. "We move through the forest and fields, looking for prey. All wolves know the scent of prey. So, since I can tell when a scent is wrong, not animal and yet not human, you think we should hunt this way?"

"That's all I've got, Igor. If you've got a better idea I'd love to hear it."

"No, I think you're right. We have two more rural addresses to check out first, but then we should do it this way. This area here is closest, we should start there. So, what will it be, known address, or the closest to town?"

Rhonda gave him a wicked grin. "Hey, I'm just the scout, you're the hunter. It's your call."

Igor looked at her, grinned, then nodded his head. Queen Sally had told Illya that someday he would lead his own pack. Perhaps it was time to start acting like an alpha. He was tired of constantly holding himself in check, playing the child he no longer felt himself to be. Besides, if he was to truly impress this amazing woman, he had to start acting like a man. "Da, known address first." He pulled on one of the gloves. "Come to me, my pretty bird."

Rhonda blushed, then laughed. "You say the sweetest things." She shimmered into the hawk and hopped onto the gloved fist he held out to her. He stroked her feathers once then stepped out and closed the door behind him.

As Igor walked out of the elevator one of the hotel personnel saw him and hurried over. "How did you get that in here? We don't allow pets in the hotel, besides, that thing should have a hood and ties on its leg so you can control it. I'm calling the police."

"I am the police," said Igor as he showed his badge. "The hawk is no danger to you; she's already been fed."

"My God, is that badge real?"

"It is, now get out of my way."

There was an air of controlled power and command in the young man's voice. The clerk stepped aside quickly, and Igor left the building, muttering to himself. He opened the car, pulled off the passenger's seat headrest, and held up his fist allowing the hawk to step onto the seat back. She had just enough head room. She watched as he tossed the backpack onto the seat.

"It has food, a first aid kit, and clothes for you should we need them," he grinned, as he programmed the first address into the GPS for directions.

Igor rolled the window down as they left town, testing the passing air for an errand scent. Suddenly he grunted and pulled over. "Like Eric says, it's better to be lucky than good," he muttered, as he stepped out and held out his fist for the hawk. "I have a scent, pretty bird. Something that should not be is near, or was not long ago. Fly now, find me the lost beast."

He swung up his arm, and with a piercing cry she leaped skyward. Igor's gaze bored into the car that passed slowly by. He recognized the man driving as one of the agents. Strapping on his weapons, he stepped into the trees and disappeared from sight, but he didn't go far. A few moments later he watched as the man parked beside the SUV and followed him into the woods.

The man in the cheap suit and street shoes had barely entered the trees when he suddenly felt a gun pressed to his back. "Don't move, don't do anything stupid, and you'll survive this day. Drop your gun slowly."

He complied. "Look, I'm a federal agent, I ..."

"You're a dead man if you move. Now easy and slow, remove and drop your backup gun."

"My backup gun?"

"I'm three paces behind you. If you breath wrong I'll shoot you. Now, the backup. Good, now your ID. Now your clothes."

"What? No fucking way I'm ..."

He gulped and swallowed hard as he felt the knife at his throat. "Jacket, shirt, and pants, on the ground now. Shoes too."

The man gulped and, as the blade left his throat, reached for his necktie. Suddenly he spun around and lashed out. His kick missed and he was staring down the barrel of a rifle that was several paces away. Igor grinned at him and lowered his aim. "Get them off or I'll shoot you in the balls."

Snarling, the man stripped to his underwear and socks. "Now, step away." Igor slid the rifle across his back, but he now held a nine-millimeter pistol on his victim. Carefully he went through the man's clothes and came up with car keys. He tossed them over.

"Now then, Mr. Federal Agent, I was born and raised in the forests of eastern Russia. Don't ever follow me into the trees again. Go back to your hotel, I'll drop off your belongings for you when I'm finished with what I have to do here. Now go." The man started away, but Igor stopped him. "Not that way, there, that way."

The man gave him a look of pure hate as he carefully picked his way back towards his car. Twice he stopped to look back, but each time Igor was there with the rifle trained on him. Swearing and cursing Igor's ancestry for several generations, he unlocked the car and drove away.

Igor turned back into the forest. He easily caught the scent again and followed it. In mere moments, he heard the cry of the hawk and, looking up, saw her circling to the left not far ahead. He picked up his pace as the hawk dropped from the sky.

Stepping into a small clearing, Igor found the hawk perched in a tree and staring at something on the ground. It was trying to crawl away and hide. The creature was trembling and terribly weak, looking like it was made up of several different animals. It whimpered in fear as he reached its side and knelt.

The bird watched as, with a look of deep compassion, Igor reached to gently cradle the creature's head in his hands. It gazed up at him with pleading eyes then nodded slightly. He gave a quick twist, there was a snapping sound, the creature relaxed fully, and then slowly morphed back into a naked woman. She was terribly thin, and many of her bones were broken.

"Oh Amy, you poor dear soul," said Rhonda, as she shimmered back to human form.

"Go back to bird form now and watch over your friend," Igor said gently. "I'll go for the body bag and contact Miss Gudrun."

"Igor, thank you for being so gentle with her. She was a good person."

"She could not have survived, sweet Ronni, you know this."

"I know, and I know you could have just shot her and walked away. You're a good man, Igor."

A sudden grin lit up his face. "Words every man loves to hear from a beautiful naked woman," he grinned.

Rhonda's mouth formed a perfect "oh", but no sound came out. She slapped his arm and morphed back into the hawk, leaping into the air then perching on a branch. As the bird glared at him from the tree he blew her a kiss then turned back towards the car.

He checked carefully, but there was no one watching, so he sent a quick text to Gudrun then took out a body bag and headed back. When he reached the body, Rhonda dropped down from the tree, shimmered into the woman, grabbed him by the collar, kissed him soundly, then stepped back. Startled, bemused, and grinning with delight, he gazed into her eyes.

She looked into those smiling eyes, silently berating herself for what she'd done, and yet aching to do it again. As though lost in a timeless moment they continued to gaze at each other, their bodies being drawn together by a force they could not deny. "Igor..."

"I dare you to do that again."

She did, more slowly this time, savoring the sweetness of it. As their lips parted she backed away then turned and leaped skyward. Bemused, delighted, and completely lost, he watched her go. Finally, he shook off the spell and turned back to the task at hand.

High above, Rhonda watched as he gently placed the woman's body in the bag, folded her arms across her chest, then straightened out her limbs before closing the bag and carrying it back to the vehicle. When he arrived, she was perched on a branch, waiting for him.

Gudrun and Kylie arrived in a new car. "Don't worry," grinned Kylie, "we lost our tail. Put her in the car now."

"What's that bundle of clothes?" asked Gudrun. Igor told the tale of the man who followed him. She laughed heartily then offered to return the bundle to the man's hotel. "I'll take care of that for you. First Kylie and I'll take the body to the crematorium, then deliver the ashes to Terry. Where will you be?"

"It's early yet, we'll continue the hunt. Ronni called the woman Amy, you can find her on the list and check her off."

Gudrun tilted her head as she gazed at him. Something had changed in Igor. The uncertainty that had marked him as young was gone. Igor now radiated a quiet confidence and strength. Whatever had happened, she believed it to be a good thing. She patted his shoulder then turned back to her own car.

Igor watched them drive away then pulled on a glove and held out his arm. The hawk swept gracefully down to land on that fist. He set her in the vehicle then got behind the wheel. "They've rented another car," he said. "I expect this is to further confuse our observers. So, pretty bird, we have a signal for when you find prey, but now we need one to show me if we are being followed, and from where.

"You wheel to the left to mark prey, perhaps a tight wheel to the right to mark a predator? Yes?" The bird gave a soft call and bobbed her head to say she understood.

They continued towards their original destination. Suddenly he smiled wickedly. "Right now, I'm the envy of all men. I'm alone in the car with a beautiful woman, and I get to do all the talking, a luxury so few men ever get to enjoy."

The hawk turned those piercing eyes on him then suddenly pecked at his arm. Laughing he leaned away. She hopped over closer to him then smacked his head with a wing. He laughed again and she sat right by his shoulder as he drove.

They arrived and Igor got out then offered his gloved hand. She hopped on, then he launched her skyward. As the hawk disappeared into the cloudless sky, an old woman came out of the house. He flashed his badge then told her they were looking for a wild animal that had escaped from a lab, he told her it was contaminated, and she shouldn't approach it.

The old woman told him she'd seen something hanging around, peering in the windows. She'd shot at it and driven it away, but she was frightened. He promised to track it down and remove it, saying he'd let her know when it was safe again. With that she went back into the house, and he entered the forest where she'd pointed out.

"SO, I HEAR YOU GOT caught with your pants down," grinned Director Compton.

"It's not funny, Boss," replied the agent, not making eye contact.

"Sure it is. Makes me feel a lot better about the shit I got on my shoes. So, where are we, people?"

"I got lucky," said another agent. "I was trailing the woman when I spotted it, some kind of a freak of nature. I ignored it until she drove away then I grabbed it. Damn thing didn't even put up a fight, it just squealed and squealed. I think it's one of the escaped people from the incident."

"Are you certain?"

"I am, sir. It's like no animal I've ever seen before. I've got it locked in my trunk for now. What do you want to do with it?"

"Sawchuk cleansed that lab. Get our people in there and refit it. They can run some tests on that thing to see what it is. Personally, I came up empty, anybody else got good news? No? Okay then, we have a change of plans.

"Barnes, it was the Russian kid who got the drop on you, right? Okay, so tomorrow we grab him and haul his ass in on a terrorist charge. He'll know what the hell Sawchuk is up to, and we'll get it out of him. I'm tired of this shit, tomorrow we go on the offensive."

"That's a bad idea, Boss." Egan Bridger was shaking his head.

Compton turned fierce eyes on him. "Oh? Why Egan, why is that a bad idea?"

"Lots of reasons," he replied easily. "First of all, Sawchuk hasn't finished the job yet. Second, if we start hauling in his people, that wife of his ..."

"You're scared of his wife?" sneered Director Compton. "Really?"

"You don't know who she is, do you, Director?"

"Enlighten me," replied Compton, the sneer still on his face.

"Her name is Gudrun Arielsdottir, born in Iceland, trained in several countries of Europe. She inherited a team of special forces mercs from her mother. They're considered the most deadly and efficient surgical strike force in the world. Sir, if you start playing rough with these people it could go seriously bad in a hurry. They call her the Angel of Death for good reason."

Compton gazed around at his agents; he didn't see a lot of people eager to take this on. "All right," he sighed. "We'll hold off for a day or two, but keep a close eye on them, and for Christ's sake, don't let them get the drop on you again. Oh, and get that creature into a cage somewhere, I don't want to be paying for a cleaning bill if it shits in your car."

Compton was still muttering to himself and nursing a whiskey as the agent with the prize reached the parking lot and realized his rental car had been stolen. It was found the next day, a burned-out husk, the prize was gone.

Preserving a Life

Terry and troops had sat silently, listening carefully to the conversation in Compton's room. As soon as they heard the man had a victim in the trunk of his car Gudrun rose, glanced at Eric, tapped Igor on the shoulder, then they silently left the room. Riding down in the elevator Igor spoke. "We're making a rescue?"

"Stealing a car," replied Eric, grinning.

Igor was impressed as they reached the other hotel's parking lot. His hearing caught the quiet weeping in the trunk of a car, but Gudrun had heard it too. She pointed it out and Eric went to work. In seconds, he was inside the car and driving away. They followed.

A short distance from the parking lot Eric stopped and popped open the trunk. Igor was there as the frightened creature began to squeal in fear. "Hush now, my friend," he soothed as he reached in to cut the bonds that were too tight. The poor creature tried to strike at him, but he gently caught the paw and patted it, then released it and cut the ties on the legs.

It tried to scramble out and escape, but it was too weak. "Hush now, I know you're frightened, but Igor won't hurt you. Igor's a friend, you'll see. You're weak, hungry too, yes? We'll find you something to eat. Come."

He scooped it easily into his arms and carried it to the car that Gudrun held open for him. He crawled into the back seat, cradling the creature in his arms. It whimpered and struggled weakly, then, as it realized how gently it was being held, snuggled into his captor's

89

arms. Igor stroked the fur on its face and cooed soothing sounds as Gudrun drove away with Eric following in the stolen car. Once they were outside of town they stopped, and Eric torched the vehicle before joining them in their car.

"So, my little friend, can you understand me?" asked Igor. To his surprise, it nodded its head. "You can? Yes, you can. Excellent. Listen carefully now, we're friends, we're here to help. We'll take you to a place of safety. There will be people there who will help you, keep you safe. Do you understand?" Again, it nodded that it understood.

"Ask her who she is," said Gudrun.

"Da. Eric, can you read out the list of people who were there that day? My friend will let me know when she hears her name." The creature shook its head no. "No? You don't know your name?"

It furrowed its brow at him and nodded. "I'm confused, my little friend."

Eric chuckled. "Perhaps we should ask him what his name is." The creature nodded eagerly.

"Ah, now I understand," grinned Igor.

Eric began to read the names. At each one the beast shook its head no until it reached Frank Isley. At that name, it nodded yes eagerly. He had been one of the students. Tears filled those large eyes as he realized these people knew he was a person and were going to help him.

Gudrun pulled in at the hangar where the plane was hidden. As Eric prepped the plane, Gudrun spoke to the creature. "Mr. Isley, we know what happened to you, and we have people working on a solution. With your permission, Eric and Igor will take you to a sanctuary where you will be kept safe and cared for. They will do all in their power to help you.

"Justine Henley is already there, so you'll have someone there you know. Like you, Justine has been changed, but she's making progress in controlling the change. Will you go?" He nodded. "Good. Igor, put Frank on the plane and stay with him until you arrive. I'll call ahead and have someone meet you there. Tell Eric to get back here as quickly as possible."

He nodded, gently lifted the creature into his arms, and then boarded the plane. Frank snuggled against him through the take off, then he brought food and slowly fed him and gave him water. Frank was asleep in his arms when the plane landed. Sally and Harald were there with Jimmy, the medic, when they landed.

Eric gave the king a report while Igor introduced Sally and Jimmy. "You go with Queen Sally and Mr. Jimmy now, Frank. They'll find you a warm safe place to sleep, yes? They'll take care of you now. I have to go back to help find the others, but I'll visit you as soon as I return." He gently patted the creature's shoulder then turned and boarded the plane once again.

IN A SMALL WINDOWLESS room, Nikka found Justine hiding. "Nikka, was it him? Was Igor here?"

"For a moment only. I didn't see him though; I was too late. They dropped off another victim of the accident. His name is Frank, I only saw him for a moment as they took him to a small room to sleep. Mr. Torvil was there and he promised to guard the door, then turned into the bear. Frank snuggled up to him and slept. He is so terribly weak, and made of many animals."

"Do you think he'll be able to master the change?"

"No."

"Nikka?"

"To change you must know, inside, who you are, what you are. How can he do that if he is made of so many? I am Nikka, girl, or wolf. You are Justine, woman or mouse, yet always Justine just as I am always Nikka, as Igor is always Igor. No, I fear he won't be able to control it, but the king will keep him safe. He won't be hunted and killed, nor will he be taken away to be put in a cage to be experimented on.

"So, now my sister Justine, if you knew Igor was coming, why did you not go out to see him? How did you know this anyway?"

"I'm not sure how I knew, but I heard the plane, and I knew he was on it. No, little sister, the next time I see Igor I want him to see me, all of me, the woman, not the frightened half mouse."

Nikka smiled. "It won't be long now. We've been talking for some time and you didn't change back. You kept your top half all girl. If you show him that he may not even notice the rest."

Justine shrieked, swept up a pillow, and began to beat Nikka with it. Suddenly Nikka stopped trying to hide from the assault and stared at her. "Oh, Justine, look. Look what you've done." Justine stopped and looked down, her lower body was whole again, all woman. She slowly ran her hands up her legs, across her abdomen, cupped her breasts, then moved up to her face. It was human.

Tears filled her eyes as she felt herself slowly change back to the half animal. Nikka had her in a hug instantly. "No, no, my sister, don't cry. You did it. It was just for a moment, but you did it, and I know what happened. Now that we're sure you can do it, we start working on holding the change where you want it to be. Yes?"

"Yes," came the soft whisper from Nikka's shoulder. "Yes, I can and I will, I have to. I want to present Igor with a whole woman when he returns, a woman who can be a woman or a mouse as she chooses, not as fate's whim dictates. I have to get control of this."

"You will, sweet Justine, my sister, you will."

Double Crossed

Igor slouched in the co-pilot's seat as the plane sped back toward Boone. "You all right?" asked Eric.

"A bit tired, no more," he replied. "It's always like this, right? Sometimes you go into battle rested and others not so much."

Eric chuckled at that. "Yes indeed. So, she wasn't there to greet you."

"What? Who?"

"Justine."

"Oh, no, I didn't expect her to be."

"But you hoped?"

"No, not so much."

"Okay, got your eye on another woman?"

"Da. Dr. Ronni makes me crazy. Yes, I liked snuggling with the little mouse, but it's a protection instinct there."

"And with Ronni?"

"Lust, pure and simple."

Eric gave a great bellowing laugh. "No, my young friend, with a woman, nothing is ever simple. Especially not with these women."

"These women?"

"It's hard enough to figure out what's going on with a normal woman. These ladies have the instincts of their animal to consider as well. Factor in your wolf and it surely will not be simple, it 'll make you crazy."

93

"Da, it has already done that. So, my comrade in arms, you have been through this before, yes? Have you any useful advice for me?"

"About the women? No, but I do have some advice that will keep you alive."

Igor was paying attention now. "Eric?"

"Women are a true delight, my young friend, and they are the reason we do what we do, but you have to be able to put those thoughts aside when you're on a mission. If you allow your thoughts to dwell on a woman, and not on your surroundings, the enemy, they can get you. You have to develop the discipline to put the thoughts of the woman aside. Enjoy her while the time is right, but put it aside when the action starts. Do you understand?"

"Yes, I do. In truth, that was why I missed the shot on that beast. Also, when that man tried to shoot me, Miss Gudrun chewed me out because I paid more attention to Ronni instead of the enemy I'd defeated."

"She was right, Igor. Next time, make the kill, then tend to your wounded."

"I know you're right, Eric. If I ever hope to become a true alpha, I must master my own thoughts and emotions."

"With the life we lead, you have to do that just to survive."

"You sound like you have experience."

"I was on my first mission, we were nearing the target, but a man and woman appeared out of nowhere. Her dress was torn and she was running away from him. I stepped out of hiding and hit him. He went down hard, but she turned and went to him, trying to protect him. I hesitated because she was so beautiful, and my mind was on my own girl back in Denmark.

"He pushed her aside and shot me. My vest took the bullet, but the sound alerted our target. There was a bad firefight and we got pushed back. Two of my brothers were killed and another badly wounded.

"You should have killed your man, Igor. If Ronni had a problem with that she's not the woman for you. Igor, the life we lead, that you will lead, will demand strength from you, especially if you aspire to be a leader.

"Look at Gudrun. She's all fun and flirty, teasing and playful when it's safe..."

"But she goes cold and efficient when we go to work. Yes, I have seen her do this. I will watch her more closely, learn what I can."

"That's the idea, little brother, learn from the best to become the best. Ah, looks like we're here." As they left the plane, Clyde was waiting. Something was up, and it wasn't good.

"Clyde, what's gone wrong now?" asked Eric.

"Compton's on the warpath," Clyde replied, as they piled into the SUV. "One of his agents got himself killed by something while you guys were gone. By our figures there are only two people left to account for and the lab has been cleared. Terry's waiting for us with the mobile lab at Justine's old cabin."

"Why there?" asked Igor.

"Because Compton's issued warrants for our arrest, all of us, and he's got the local police on the hunt."

To the surprise of both men, Igor suddenly took charge, the natural alpha coming to the fore. "Turn back, Clyde. Eric, get the plane back to the Lair, we dare not let Compton have it. Report to the king about what's happened here. Clyde, you go back with Eric, this is a different mission now. I'll go to the cabin; with luck they'll still be there."

Startled, Clyde looked to Eric, who nodded. "Do it, Clyde." He agreed and pulled a fast U-turn.

IGOR ARRIVED AT THE cabin to find it empty. The mobile lab was gone, the rental cars were gone, and so were his people. Before he could do anything, there came the cry of a hawk. He glanced up to see the bird plummet towards the ground. It morphed into Rhonda as it reached him. She fell into his arms, sobbing. As he held her gently, Gudrun appeared from the trees.

"Where is Eric?"

"I sent him back to the Lair, Clyde with him," replied Igor. "We dare not let Compton get his hands on that plane. Now, what has happened here?"

"We retreated here," said Ronni, as she got control of her emotions. "The sheriff and his men arrived shortly after. I flew and the rest fled into the trees. They caught Clara, and then Terry gave himself up to distract them. Gudrun and Georg escaped. I lost track of them."

"Gudrun, do you know where Georg is?"

"I'm here," he called, as he exited the trees.

Igor took Rhonda by the shoulders and gazed into her eyes. "Be strong now, my lady hawk. I need you to be strong. Miss Gudrun, they've taken Mr. Terry and Miss Clara. I know you can find them. Take Georg with you and get them back. There are still two more mutant animals for us to find. Ronni and I will do this. Does this work for you?"

"It does," she replied, her eyes hard.

Igor tossed her the car keys. "Go. When you have them, find a way back to the Lair. Ronni and I will finish our end then do the same."

Gudrun nodded then tossed him the backpack. "Ronni's clothes, some food, and a spare gun," she said. "Georg, let's go." They leaped aboard the car then sped away.

"I wouldn't want to be Director Compton right now," sighed Igor, as he turned back to Rhonda. He took her in his arms and held her gently. "I'm dead on my feet. Can you watch while I rest then we can take up the hunt?"

"Yes, of course. Igor, are you okay?"

"I'm just tired. A few hours sleep and I'll be ready to hunt."

He kissed her cheek and loosened his arms around her, but she took his face in her hands then kissed him soundly again. She stepped back and gazed into his eyes for a moment then leaped skyward. Somewhat bemused and delighted, he watched as she perched in a tall tree near the back of the cabin. With a nod of approval, Igor went to the back, morphed into the wolf, then curled up beneath her tree.

The day was well along when he awakened, shook himself, then changed back and began pulling on his clothes. He heard the rush of wings then Rhonda was standing beside him. "Quickly, Igor, they're coming." With that she leaped into the air and flew away again. He swept up the backpack and vanished into the forest.

A police car pulled up to the cabin and two deputies got out. One opened the back door and a police dog jumped to the ground. "Okay, Duke, find 'em. Go find 'em, boy." The dog snuffled about for a minute then set out into the trees.

Ahead of the dog, Igor fled at a run. He ran for tougher terrain, but he knew there was no way to shake the dog from his trail, that wasn't what he was trying to do, he just wanted distance from the men. When he was certain he had a good lead, he stopped running and morphed into the wolf. The dog broke from the bushes and yelped as it leaped aside. It wasn't a human facing him.

The dog whimpered and dropped to his belly as the wolf, head down and snarling, advanced. It stood over the cowering dog until it urinated and whimpered again, looking away. The huge beast growled once then trotted into the trees and disappeared. A short while later the two men saw their dog returning, his head down and his tail tucked between his legs.

"Shit, Duke, what happened to you? What happened, boy?" The dog was terrified, and the handler tried to sooth him. "Wonder what happened to him? A bear, maybe?"

"Hell no, we've both seen him face down a bear before. Must have been something though. I never seen him so scared before. Come on,

Duke, find 'im, find 'im boy." The dog just hung its head and whimpered, refusing to take up the trail. Bemused and troubled they turned back towards their car.

"I just don't know what could have scared him like that."

"Me either, but I'll tell you true, whatever the hell it was, I don't want to meet up with it. To hell with this, let's get him back to the vet, get him something to calm him down."

Off in the trees, a beast from the past stood watching the sky as a large hawk circled down carrying something huge in its talons. The bird dropped the backpack to him then landed and morphed into the woman. "Damn, that thing is heavy."

The wolf shimmered back into the man. "Thank you, pretty bird, but you shouldn't take a risk like that. I could go back for it. Did you see the men? Have they gone?"

"Yes, they've gone," she replied, pulling on the jeans he tossed to her. "You scared that poor dog shitless."

He chuckled at that. "Yes, but I didn't hurt him. He might fight a man or a bear, but he's canine like me, he recognized a more powerful alpha and submitted. It carried some of the scent he was following, so he knew he had to stop tracking me."

She nodded thoughtfully. "Igor, you've changed in the past couple of days. What's going on with you?"

"Something is changing inside me, sweet Ronni. I feel stronger, more powerful, more driven to take control, and it's all your fault."

"My fault? How did it get to be my fault?"

His eyes twinkled with mischief as he replied. "You kissed me, and my world changed forever."

"That's sweet, and it's the old Igor I love, but you're avoiding the question. Talk to me."

"Da, I tease, but I tell the truth also. Queen Sally has told grandfather that I will someday lead my own pack. I'm at the age when a young alpha will make a challenge, or will leave the pack to create his own. Your nearness has triggered those emotions in me, but they nearly got us both killed, and I fought them.

"Eric says that I can do as I please, but when we are at work on a mission, I must put aside all thoughts of a mate and focus. He's right, I must master this if I'm to survive and protect a mate, a pack."

"Igor, what are you saying to me?"

He looked deeply into her eyes. "I will speak plainly, my pretty bird. You make me crazy, in a good and special way, but I need to keep my thoughts off you, and on the task at hand when we are working, like we are now. I need to be able to focus."

"Okay..."

"Ronni, the wolf mates for life."

"So does the hawk, Igor. What are you saying here?" Her eyes locked onto his, hoping, imploring, daring to hope as her heart ached for the answer she longed to hear and knew she shouldn't want.

"I like your kisses?"

The merriment in his eyes was infectious and she grinned in return, her hopes rising. "Is that all you like?"

"I especially like it that you're always naked when you do it."

That made her laugh. "What are you saying to me? Igor, what are we doing here?"

"I'm not sure, Ronni, my pretty bird. I think it might be some sort of strange human mating ritual."

Again, she laughed, then sobered. "There's something you should know."

"You are immortal like Mr. Torvil and the great mother, Miss Ella. You will stay young and beautiful while I grow old and eventually return to the great forest."

"Clara told you?"

"What? No. No, Ronni, Miss Clara said nothing of this to me. Those of you who came to the change from the exploding stone are immortal, Miss Ella, Torvil, and the vampires who sprang from them.

The Children of the Wolf came to the change by a different path. I will live a very long time, perhaps twice the age of a human, but I will age and, once killed, I cannot return as you can.

"There are many things that stand in the way of such a mating, my Ronni. Grandfather will object for certain."

"What? Why would Illya ..."

"No pups, pretty bird. The immortals have no pups. The vampires can make other vampires, but that's all. Torvil has no children, nor has Ella. Grandfather wants to rebuild the packs as quickly as possible. He has already told me to find a human woman to mate."

"Is that why you were showing off for the household staff back at the Lair?"

"Yes, but I fear I must incur the anger of my pack's alpha."

"Oh? Why?"

"I kissed one of those girls. It was nice, but it didn't set my soul on fire like your kiss does."

"Oh man, you sure know how to say the right thing at just the right time." She fairly purred as she snuggled into his arms. Sliding her arms around his neck, she brought her lips to his. "Igor, are you certain about this?" she asked as their lips parted.

"Huh? What? I'm sorry, but I can't seem to remember my name right now. Who are you, amazing woman?"

"Stop it, you fool," she laughed, as she lightly slapped his arm. "Igor, do you truly want me?"

"I do, my pretty bird, but only if you want me too. If not, I will try to let you go, but I fear my wolf has already chosen you."

She hugged him tight enough to break bone. "My hawk has chosen you as well. I'm all yours, Igor, now and forever if you want me. Promise me."

"I swear it, sweet woman, we have bonded, both our avatar animals mate for life. Hawk and wolf are as one now, forever. Someone else will have to make the pups to increase the numbers of our people."

"Igor, I know we have to figure out what to do next, but can we stay right here for a while longer, just like this?"

"No, we should be on the move, we can't stay here. Don't even think about kissing me again to make me forget my own name."

"I wouldn't dream of distracting you," she breathed, as she brought her lips to his once again. This time he pulled her tightly to him, holding her there, claiming her as his one and only mate.

They slept through the night and arose early. The wolf shook himself then shimmered back into the man. She yawned and stretched then rose and kissed his cheek. "Thanks for getting all furry to keep me warm."

"All my pleasure, my pretty bird."

"So, what's on our agenda today, my fine bold man?"

"I like the sound of that," he grinned. "So, first we eat what food is left in the pack, then we store our clothes and weapons here. Miss Gudrun will get Mr. Terry and Miss Clara back, our task is to find the last two people on the missing list, do whatever we must, then make our way back to the Lair. We will hunt as wolf and hawk. We have tried this the human way and failed. Now we trust our true nature to get the job done."

"Igor, the plane's gone, and so are half our people. What will we do if we find one who we can save?"

"If that happens we'll take them home through the forest. I know your soft loving heart, my lady hawk. I will not kill unnecessarily. However, it will be necessary to a certain extent."

"Igor?"

"We will need food, to keep up our strength. Both hawk and wolf will have to hunt for food as well as for the missing ones."

Rhonda sighed. "I guess you're right, my love. I don't like doing it, but you're right. Igor, I know that in a pack the alpha's word is law. Whatever will you do with this fiercely independent hawk you've chosen for a mate?"

"Hmm, I expect I'll have an exciting life, yeah?"

Her eyes twinkled with merriment. "Oh yes, I can guarantee that. Seriously now. How do we do this?"

He instantly became serious and took charge. "We return to where we found Amy, then we begin our hunt. For you, wide circles to the right, small to the left to mark the target, or small to the right to mark a predator we fear."

"Got it," she said, as she stuffed the wrappers and her clothes into the backpack. He morphed into the wolf and trotted away. She put his clothes with hers then hid the pack before leaping into the cloudless sky. A moment later he looked up to see the hawk making a lazy circle to the right.

No Cage Can Hold

While the wolf and hawk confessed their love for each other, Terry Sawchuk and Clara Bynes were facing a far less pleasant evening. They were being held in a private building, not a police station. Compton ignored Clara for the most part, focusing all his energy on Terry.

Terry sat in a chair in the middle of an empty room. He was naked and held fast by heavy restraints. Compton sat facing him, a sneer of contempt on his face. "Not so fucking arrogant now, are you Sawchuk?"

Terry didn't answer, he just kept looking around the room, making a mental note of everything he saw. He could feel Gudrun getting closer and knew it wouldn't be long before he was free again. Compton's men would be waiting for her with orders to shoot to kill, but they had no real idea what they were dealing with.

Suddenly Compton leaned closer and slammed his fist into Terry's face. "Pay attention, Sawchuk, I'm talking here."

Terry spat blood from his split lip into Compton's face. The man shouted and leaped to his feet, wiping at his face with the handkerchief from his jacket pocket. "You fucking son of a bitch, Sawchuk." He started kicking at the man bound in the chair, knocking it over.

Egan Bridger got between them, pushing Compton back. "Hey, hey, cut it out. What the hell's the matter with you?"

103

"Me? What the hell's the matter with you? Who the hell do you think you are, putting your hands on me? Get the hell away from me while I interrogate the prisoner."

"You're way over the line here, Director. We had no reason to arrest this man, we hired him ourselves to clean up a mess we couldn't handle. Now you drag him in and assault him? Shit, you didn't even ask him a question. You need to get a grip."

"What's the matter with you, Egan, you've gone soft on Sawchuk for some reason?"

"I haven't gone soft on anybody, sir, but you're getting way off track here, you've crossed the line. We have nothing on Sawchuk, and we need him to finish cleaning up this mess."

"Oh yes, and then he just disappears again to commit treason and sabotage the nation? Dammit, Egan, you know as well as I do he's using foreign nationals on American soil. He's a traitor."

"There's no proof of any of that, Director," replied Egan, as he stepped back from his boss. "What we do know for certain is that, over the past number of years, Sawchuk and his people have stopped a number of situations from getting out of control.

"Sir, you pulled him back and put Mendez in control of Sawchuk's team before you sent them against that maddened serial killer. Look what happened there, two men got killed and Terry had to take over anyway to get the job done."

"Yes, and there was an incident in the customs warehouses as well as a destroyed embassy."

"We have no proof Sawchuk was involved in either of those actions, besides, the serial killer, a foreign national himself, disappeared forever. Sir, I've worked with this man before and one thing I can say for certain, Terry Sawchuk is a patriot to the core."

The other three agents in the room were staying well back, just listening. "Sir, in honesty, I've never quite understood your aggressive dislike for this man. He was a fine agent, an asset to the department. I just don't get it."

"Aggressive dislike? Aggressive dislike? I hate the fucker."

"Why?"

"It's a personal issue, none of your goddamned business."

"I stopped him from torturing a female prisoner," said Terry, as he spat out more blood. "Compton got his promotions from political allies of his father, not for his ability. He's a chickenshit and a bully with no talent. He's a liability to the department and the country."

"Fuck you, Sawchuk ..."

He lunged at the bound prisoner, but Egan stepped in his path and held him back. "Sir, you need to cool off."

"Fine, then we'll just leave him where he is and go back to the hotel for a good night's rest in a comfortable bed." Egan bent to Terry and stood the chair back up with him still in it. "Leave him. I said leave him, Egan, unless you want a transfer to the north pole. Come on." Reluctantly, Egan turned and followed the others out.

As soon as Clara heard the cars drive away she set to work. Placing her back to the wall where the camera couldn't see her, she began to fiddle with her bra. In a moment, she had a wire to work with. The locked door opened easily to give her access to a corridor. Only one other door was locked, and she swiftly opened it.

Terry was in the middle of the empty room, his lips swollen and bleeding. She held her finger to her lips for silence. Leaving the door slightly ajar, she continued exploring. Clara grinned as she found what she was looking for, a single night watchman, sitting at a monitoring system. He was fast asleep.

Pulling a pad from her bra and snapping the capsule inside it, she slipped in behind him and pressed the foam tightly to his face. Startled, he began to thrash about, but instantly melted to the floor, the fumes from the activated pad doing a swift job of rendering him unconscious.

"Sorry, buddy. You'll have one hell of a headache in the morning, but I need to borrow your gun and car keys."

Clara ran back to Terry and cut his bonds. She passed him the first aid kit and the gun she'd taken from the guard room, and then forced open the locker to find his clothes. He dressed swiftly then they fled to the parking lot. Clara pressed the button on the key chain and an older model car chirped.

Grinning she tossed him the keys. "Your bond will direct you to Gudrun. Get us out of here, Terry."

"Yes ma'am, I work as we speak," he replied, as they jumped in the car and sped away. "Clara, have I told you lately you're a genius?"

"Yes, but do it again. I love to hear it."

Terry laughed. "Woman, you're a genius, and I'm sure glad you're on our side."

"THIS IS THE PLACE, but he's no longer here," said Gudrun.

"The scent is strong, and I smell blood, Terry's blood," replied Georg. "Do we investigate?"

"We do, but quickly. Come." Gudrun led the way inside. A quick scout showed them the downed watchman and the empty cells. "Terry was bound to this chair and tortured. I can smell his blood and Compton's hate."

"Yes, but Clara was also in this room. I know her well enough to know a cell could never hold her. I believe she waited until the others left, then she set him free and they escaped. They probably stole that watchman's car and went looking for us."

"Agreed, and I know just where they'll go. Come."

They ran back to the car and sped away. Gudrun talked as she drove. "We always have three different rendezvous points in case a mission goes wrong. One for an escaped target, one for mission failure, and another in case of capture then escape. I know exactly where Terry will go, in fact I can feel us getting closer.

The cafe was closed for the night, but, as they pulled into the parking lot, Terry and Clara stepped out from behind the building. They got in the car, Terry beside Gudrun and Clara in the back seat, cuddled in Georg's arms. Gudrun kissed Terry then drove away.

"Terry, what the hell happened?"

"Compton lost it all over me," he sighed, "but Egan got in his face and calmed him down a bit. He'll have to watch his back from now on, he'll be on Compton's hit list for sure after this one. Once everybody went home Clara broke out and rescued me."

"I told you so, Gudrun." chuckled Georg.

"Yes you did," smiled Gudrun. "Clara, you're a far more resourceful ally than I knew. I apologize for underestimating you."

Clara laughed at that. "Thank you, Gudrun. In truth, I work at that, being underestimated. I'm a lab geek. Everybody ignores us. Those morons took my handbag then threw me in a cell without a body search. I wear special clothing when in the field. Lock picks, weapons, methods of rendering people unconscious, that sort of thing."

"Really? Clara, would you consider making me a special wardrobe?"

"I'll get started as soon as I'm back in my own lab," she grinned.

"Then that's where we'll go."

"Gudrun my darling, what's going on?"

"We're done here, Terry. I'm taking you home, picking up my crew, and then I'm going after Compton."

"Honey..."

"No, he double crossed us. He goes down."

"Not arguing that, sweetheart, but we've still got a mission to finish for the king. There's still two more people to account for."

"Igor's got that."

"Igor? He's a rookie with a world of potential, but... all right, tell me what's going on."

"We've got another problem, that's what's going on," sighed Georg.

Terry turned in the seat to look at him. "Talk to me, Georg, what does that mean?"

"Igor and Dr. Ronni will bring trouble to us soon. Their animal avatars are maturing, ready to mate."

"You've seen them, Terry," said Gudrun. "She flirts and coos at him, and he drools every time she gets near."

"Her attentions have triggered his alpha nature," said Georg. "He took command, sent us after you, and said they would take care of the last two people on the list. He said they'd find their own way back to the Lair."

"Okay, and this is bad because?"

"The drive is on him now," replied Georg. "He'll hunt in wolf form, he'll travel in wolf form, and when he reaches the castle he'll challenge for dominance. Illya wants to rebuild the people as quickly as possible. He has commanded all of us to find human mates to bring many pups and to increase the gene pool.

"By now Igor has claimed Ronni, both hawk and wolf mate for life, and she is barren."

"Barren? What makes you say that?" asked Clara.

"All the immortals are barren. Torvil made no children, Ella has born no children, nor have any of the vampires."

"What makes you say she's immortal?"

"Clara, my beloved, you know this to be true. Ronni came to the change with the exploding stone, as did Ella and Torvil. Ella's change also involved much blood, and so she can make more vampires, all immortal, all barren. Justine will be immortal as well. Only the Children of the Wolf are not. We came to the change by another road. We are long lived, but still mortal."

"Is he right, Clara?" asked Terry.

"Yes, Terry, I believe he is."

"Are you sure about Igor and Ronni?"

"We are, sweetie," sighed Gudrun.

"Well shit, that throws a wrench into the works," sighed Terry, as he settled back in his seat. "So, what do we do about this? Is it safe for us to leave the two of them to get this done?"

"Oh yes," said Georg. "Igor is alpha now, and he's given his word to do this. He'll hunt them and deal with the bodies."

"How?" asked Terry. "How will he deal with the bodies?"

"I don't know," replied Georg, "but I can guess. He will hunt them, probably kill then mangle the body once it returns to human form. The dead human will be found and identified as a dead human."

"Oh, that's not good at all," said Clara. "They'll use DNA to identify the victim, but there'll be animal DNA mixed in, raising questions."

"Shit. This is so not good. What do we do now?" grumbled Terry.

"What do you want to do, lover?" asked Gudrun.

"This is my case. The king expects me to get it done, and I promised to do just that. I want to go back and find Igor, help him to dispose of the bodies. If he brings them to us we can have them cremated then I can deliver the ashes and close the case.

"Besides, if I'm still seen in the area, Compton might make another play for me. It'll be easier for you to take him down. You leave me here, take Clara back to the castle, pick up your team then take Compton out."

"You want me to kill him?"

Terry didn't like having to kill anyone, but his first loyalty was to his family. However, he wasn't happy about having been tortured either. "I'd rather do it myself, but with him gone, Egan Bridger will inherit the job, and we can work with him. If we leave Compton alive he'll start probing at the Lair, its people, the whole town. He's as big a threat to us as Krebs was, worse even. Yes, it's personal with him, but not with me. Take him out, and I don't care how you do it."

"Consider it done, my love. Will you be all right on your own until I get back?"

"I will. I'll stay out of sight, make contact with Igor, then stay low until you get back. Deal?"

"Deal. You want Georg to stay with you?"

"No. If Igor's that dangerous right now I think the two of them should stay far apart for a while. I'll muddle through on my own."

"So be it. Where do you want me to drop you off? At the cabin?"

"No. Drop me at the hotel, I want to clear our rooms. I'll go to the spot where the forest is closest to the old lab. Igor will probably start his search there. I'm hoping he'll catch my scent and make contact."

"It's a good plan, Terry," agreed Georg, "but be extremely careful. A young alpha can be somewhat unpredictable."

"Good to know," grinned Terry, as Gudrun pulled over to let him out. Bold as brass he walked into the building and asked for his key. Shaking her head and grinning, Gudrun drove away.

"Where are we going now, Gudrun?" asked Clara. "The Lair is a long way north of here and you're driving south."

"I know. Compton will look for you and Terry heading north. I want to find a place where Eric can put that damn plane down."

An hour later she pulled over and took out her phone. "Eric, it's Gudrun. Equip for a cleansing mission. Bring everything we'll need and find me at these coordinates. Yes, we'll need Vassily and Jimmy both. We'll be waiting."

While Gudrun waited impatiently for her crew to arrive, Terry packed and checked out for the whole group. Compton's men had searched everything, but left the mess. Terry called for a bell hop to help him get everything downstairs, then rented another vehicle. Once it was loaded, he drove away.

The agent followed Terry to the cafe parking lot, then watched as he went to the door, jimmied it open then went inside. As the agent followed him inside, Terry struck. He left the woman lying unconscious on the floor then went back outside and drove away. He took out the agent's phone and called a special number.

"Who are you and how did you get this number?"

"It's me, Kylie. You still loose?"

"Oh yeah, morons. What's the plan?"

"You in a rental or a stolen?"

"Rental."

"They get anything?"

"Nope, I still have my laptop and disposed of everything else. What's the plan?"

"Go home, Kylie. Dump the rental and take the bus or train north. Use a fake ID to buy the ticket."

"Understood." She hung up then destroyed the phone. So did he.

While Kylie headed north, Terry used the downed agent's credit card to rent storage then moved everything into it from the car. He then drove to Compton's hotel and ordered breakfast. He was just finishing up as Compton and Egan entered. Terry winked at Egan, saluted Compton then walked out through the kitchen.

With gun drawn, Compton blasted through the door and out the back of the building. Terry stepped out from behind the shelves, grinned at the startled staff, then left through the dining room. Compton returned empty handed and swearing profusely into the phone. He was arranging a manhunt. His jaw dropped as he glanced out the window to see Terry break into his rental car and drive away.

Knowing Compton would be on the phone to the local cops instantly, he drove around the block then got out and hailed a taxi. The cab dropped him beside his own rental and drove away. Terry went to the place he hoped to find Igor then hid his car on an ATV trail.

Exhausted, Terry settled down beneath a tree for a nap, well out of sight of his hidden car. He awakened late in the day with a wolf and hawk watching, protecting his hiding place.

He yawned and stretched then sat up. "So, what's new, guys?"

They both transformed to human form. It was Rhonda who spoke first. "I'll watch, you bring the boss up to speed." Igor nodded his agreement as she leaped into the sky and began a lazy circle overhead.

"Igor?"

The young man brought his attention back to Terry. "Forgive me, Terry. I seem to be struggling with a hormone issue these days."

"The girl sets the old alpha hormones on fire, does she?"

"She makes me crazy," he sighed. "I was incomplete without her."

"So you've bonded."

"Da. Is that a problem?"

"Not for me."

"Okay, so, since there is no one else here, I won't worry about that now. I see that Miss Gudrun found you."

"Yes. Clara had already rescued me, we met up with Gudrun and Georg later. They've gone back to the Lair to get Gudrun's attack team. She's going after Compton."

"But not you?"

"No. Gudrun said you'd taken control of finding the last two on the list. I came to help."

"I need no help."

"Didn't say you did, Igor. I hung back to show myself and hold Compton's attention on me, that'll keep him in the area, easier for Gudrun to find. I also want to help you dispose of the bodies if necessary. If you leave them as a wolf kill the humans will hunt you. They might also use DNA testing then start asking questions. If you find them and have to make a kill, I'll dispose of the body just like the rest. We return the ashes, and the families get come closure."

"And Compton?"

"Gudrun's problem. He's as good as dead already."

"His men?"

"My problem. You chose the hunt, that's yours to deal with. So, can we work together?"

"Of course. Why are you acting like I'll bite your head off?"

"Georg suggested I should be wary around a young alpha."

Igor laughed and relaxed. "Da, he was not wrong, Terry. I'm a special problem, I know. When I was held by Krebs they trained me to fight and kill. They reached past the natural instincts to touch something in me that should not have been touched. When I fight, I become savage, too savage, I kill. They also gave us other things, drugs in our food. My wolf is bigger and stronger than the others, perhaps bigger than it should be."

"Then you have to be stronger as well, Igor, you know this."

"I do. Miss Ella has worked with me."

"Oh?"

"I know what I am, Terry, and I know what was done to me, what I was made into. A killing machine, an animal beyond savage. I also know the Great Mother taught the vampires to control the killing lust. I asked, and she agreed to teach me."

"So that's why she didn't want you coming on this mission."

"She was unsure if I was ready. I was doing fine until Ronni kissed me."

Terry laughed at that. "Oh yeah, that'll mess you up all right. So, how are you doing now?"

"Fine. I was slowly losing control, but we talked, we bonded, and I felt something inside me settle. I'm still a bit edgy, but I'm getting the control back."

"I have to say, Igor, you had full control when we found Justine."

"She was so like little Nikka, so frightened. All I wanted to do was protect her. That also triggered my alpha. I said that Ronni and I would travel back through the forest to give me more time to work on the control."

"We'll leave that up to you. Just tell me where we stand."

"Excuse me?"

"I serve the king, we all do..."

"Ah, I see. I too serve the king, Terry. I do, and I will. He made you commander of this mission; I will honor that. Orders?"

"Go with your plan, you've got it mapped," grinned Terry.

"How do we stay in contact?"

"I'll keep checking back. If you have something for me, meet me here." The young man nodded then transformed back into the wolf and trotted away. Terry went back to his car.

KING HARALD STRODE up to the plane as the men loaded their equipment on board. "Eric, talk to me."

"Sire, it's all gone to hell as far as I know. The government man, Compton, double crossed us. We were nearly finished when he suddenly arrested Terry and Clara. They tried to grab us all, but the rest of us escaped. Actually, Terry gave himself up to save Clara.

"Compton tortured Terry, but his aide called him off. As soon as the prison was empty except for a single guard, Clara broke free, took down the guard, and released Terry. They met up with Gudrun and Georg."

"And the plan is?"

"Igor and Ronni are still on point; they'll finish up the original mission. Gudrun's called for a full tactical. The target is Compton."

"She feels this is necessary?"

"He'll never stop hunting for Terry, which means ..."

"He'll start poking around here. As usual, Gudrun is on top of the situation. Now, what aren't you telling me?"

"Apparently, Ronni's hawk got broody just as Igor's wolf matured. She flirted with him and that triggered the alpha in him. Georg thinks there's trouble brewing."

"There always is with teenage hormones," sighed the king. "Eric, tell Gudrun to do this as quietly ... oh hell, she knows better than I do how this must be done. You go, I'll talk to Sally and Illya to see what we do about the teenagers. Good hunting."

"Thank you, Sire," grinned Eric, as he climbed to the cockpit of the plane and started the checklist. Within moments the plane was in the air.

An Alpha Awakened

They lay together in a bed of sweet smelling grasses. Rhonda could feel the tension in him and snuggled closer. "Talk to me, Igor. What's bugging you?"

"It was something Terry said."

"Oh? What did he say to upset you?"

"The others know that we've bonded, sweet Ronni. They know you triggered my alpha, and they're frightened."

"Frightened? Why?"

"They fear I will kill grandfather."

"What? What the hell would make them think that? A challenge rarely ends in death of either wolf, no matter who is successful, besides, you said you'd just leave his pack, so no challenge or battle."

"Ronni, they know what was done to me by Krebs. They know that he gave us drugs to make us bigger and stronger, more savage. They don't know if I can control the emotion of battle. They don't trust me, and they're frightened of what I might do, now that my alpha is awake."

"Oh god, Igor, you said Ella ..."

"Yes, the Great Mother has been teaching me, but she wanted to be near when the alpha awakened, so she could help me."

"And she's not here, so the rest are concerned."

"Yes, but I don't need her to be."

"Are you sure?"

"That man with a gun attacked you, yet I didn't kill him. You asked me not to, yes, but I didn't need that, I found I had the control that

116

day. Ronni, I would not have spoken for your heart if I wasn't certain I could control the beast within. I won't harm Illya, nor will I challenge the king. I, Igor, am in control here, not the alpha, or the wolf nature, but me."

"But they don't know that, how could they?"

"Right, and that's the problem. I'm not sure what we'll be facing when we return to the castle."

"Relax, my lover, we'll deal with that when we get there. We'll move into Bill's barn if we have to."

He chuckled at that. "Da, I can be the guard wolf and you can be the veterinarian in residence." That made her laugh.

Once again, Rhonda awakened with the dawn, snuggled into the wolf. She lovingly stroked his warm fur then yawned and sat up, tousling her hair. He opened his eyes then stood and shook before transforming back to the man. "You know, I'm starting to like sleeping out in the open with the big bad wolf to keep me warm."

He laughed as he pulled her close for a kiss. "Ah, my pretty bird, I think you were always a wild woman."

"No, I wasn't. Human society doesn't really encourage girls to be wild."

"Well, I like my wild woman."

"And I'm thrilled that you do... Igor, what is it?"

"Better to be lucky than good," he replied. "I just caught a scent, woman and not woman. It is near."

"And so, to work. Be careful, my love." With that the hawk leaped into the air and was soon circling high overhead, fierce eyes searching for anything unusual on the ground.

Igor had transformed into the wolf and trotted away from where he sensed the creature to be. Once in the trees he circled around downwind and caught a strong scent. A short time later he found it. High above, the hawk was circling to the left.

Something that looked like part alligator and part possum with human arms and hands pressed her back against a tree as the wolf found her. It hissed a warning. High overhead Rhonda felt fear course through her as Igor transformed back into the man.

"Do not fear me, beautiful woman, Igor is here to help you. I know what has happened and I can help you." He relaxed his posture and spoke softly. "I do, I know what's happened to you. I know you're frightened. Igor is here to help. Easy now. Can you understand my words? If you can just nod your head."

The only response was another warning hiss. "Please, beautiful lady, talk to Igor. Just nod your head if you can understand me. I know what's happened to you. I have met the others. Justine is a friend. I have taken her to a safe place, and I can do the same for you. We have people there ..."

With startling speed it attacked, but the powerful jaws snapped shut on empty air. Spinning about and hissing, the creature faced the enemy. Igor was gone and the huge dire wolf was there. Again, the beast attacked, but the wolf faded away from the mighty jaws. The beast turned to see the man standing several paces away.

"Please, sweet woman, don't make Igor do this. You can understand me, I know you can. Just nod your head yes. Let us help you."

It threw dirt at his face then charged. He leaped aside, avoiding both the dirt and the attack. "So be it. I will be as swift as possible as I end your pain." It snapped at him again and he changed as he leaped away.

The wolf darted in. The beast snapped at him, but the great jaws missed. The wolf grabbed the beast by the back of the neck and bit down hard. Bone snapped under the power of those jaws as the wolf shook his victim then dropped it. The hawk swooped down beside him and together they transformed as they watched the body change to that of a woman and lay still.

"I tried, my pretty bird."

"I know. I saw. You had no choice, Igor. Trudy is at peace now."

"Yes. Her mind was lost to the terror, I couldn't reach her. Now you must do all the work."

"I know. I'll locate a road nearby then let Terry know where to find us."

He nodded and she flew away. Igor sighed as he watched her hunting, then she let out a piercing cry and flew west. He spoke to the dead woman even as he lifted her body to his shoulder. "I'm so sorry, Miss Trudy. I would like to allow you more dignity, but I can't. I must carry you to a place where you can rest with your family."

With the dead woman on his shoulder, he started west. An hour later he came upon a dirt road and laid the body down under a tree then sat beside it. He had a long wait. The sun was just setting when he heard the vehicle. Rhonda alit and transformed into the woman as Terry got out of the car.

Igor was on his feet, nose in the air. "Terry, is that pizza I smell?"

"Yep. I thought you both might be hungry. Any takers?"

"You're a godsend, Terry," laughed Rhonda as she opened the boxes. "My sweet lord, and root beer too?"

"You know the rules, Ronni, no alcohol when you're flying."

"Ha, ha, very funny. I'll forgive you just because you brought us food. Igor, save me another piece of that."

Smiling, Terry pulled a body bag out of the back of the car and gently laid the corpse in it. He put her in the trunk then closed the lid. "Well done, folks, well done."

"Igor tried to reason with her, Terry."

"I believe you, Ronni. I'm sure he took way too many chances before he gave up and did the deed. I'll take her to the crematorium then deliver the ashes to her family. There's only Arlo Graves left on Justine's list. Once you guys have that under control we'll get together and make a new plan."

"Once our part is finished, Ronni and I will head home through the forest."

"That may not be necessary, Igor."

"It wasn't a request. We need the time together."

Terry sighed and allowed his shoulders to relax completely. He leaned back against the car as he spoke. "Okay, let's do some of this now. First, that attitude is going to cause no end of trouble at the Lair, and you know it. Get a grip on that. Second, I know you're expecting trouble there and just want to let everybody cool their jets before you get home.

"So, here's what I suggest. You find the last one and we deal with that, then we work together to make a new plan. Right now, you're working with a small bit of information. When Gudrun gets back she'll have more intel for you, so will Eric. I'll call ahead as well. Before we go back to the Lair we'll be a lot better prepared than you will be if you just run off into the woods."

Igor gave him a hard look, but Terry ignored it and went on. "Look at the whole thing, Igor. You need the protection of the Lair, and the Lair needs you as well. If you run away, Ella will be sent after you, Ella and Torvil as well as Gudrun. You may be tough, but you're not that tough.

"Think about this. Tell me what you want to have happen here, and I'll do my best to help you."

"Why would you, Terry?"

"Because you're part of my crew, you're one of my people, and because I'm a friend. I was there when we brought you out of the slave pens. Look, you two are all gooey-eyed and in love, I know how good that feels. However, you're expecting trouble when we get back. There'll be some stress for sure, and a few issues to deal with, but we'll work on that together."

"Terry?"

"We work for the king, we all do. I lead most of the missions, except when it's an assassination, then Gudrun leads. As soon as we started this mission I saw the weakness in our armor."

"Weakness?" asked Rhonda.

"Yes, Ronni, weakness. We all work best in an urban environment. Oh yes, we can all function in the wild, but not as good as you two. You guys are a team, and out here you're way ahead of the rest of us, especially when you work together.

"Gundrun and I talked about it, and she said you'd be better as an independent scout, Ronni. I'm thinking Igor's small pack will make a real asset to any mission outside the pavement."

"A team within a team? A pack within a pack?"

"Yes, Igor my friend, that's what I mean. I'm not showing dominance here, that's not my thing. I'm all about getting the job done, done right, and as quietly as possible."

"I see what you mean, it makes sense to me, Terry. This could work."

"I'll personally speak to the king for you. Illya acknowledges him, so I'm guessing you'll have no problem, and neither will he."

"Da. Grandfather will be the problem. All right, we finish the hunt then we make a plan, yes?"

"Absolutely," grinned Terry, relief clear in his voice. "Now, I'll take this lady to her final rest and let you two carry on."

They watched him drive away then Rhonda turned to Igor. "What's going through your mind, sweetheart?"

"Mr. Terry makes sense, and it was he who led the wolves into battle when we were liberated. Grandfather did not challenge him, and I need to remember that. The drives of the alpha are strong, but Igor must be stronger, like the vampires."

"Like the vampires?"

"Yes. The blood lust, the drive to kill, is very strong, and always there, but they control it. I must do the same with the drives of the alpha. Sweet Ronni, there is so much more I wish to learn. Mr. Tommy is a wizard with electronics, and he will teach me. Miss Gudrun is the world's greatest warrior, and she is willing to teach me.

"Grandfather is beyond wise, and the greatest leader the Children of the Wolf have ever known. There is so much I can learn from him, if I can convince him to teach me."

"And it all depends on your ability to control the alpha drives within you. Igor my love, I've seen you do this several times. You have control, my love. Use it."

"Perhaps it looks that way," he sighed, as he sank to the ground and patted the space beside him.

She lowered herself beside him and cuddled into his arms. "What do you mean, looks that way?"

"Krebs did things to us, injected things into our bodies to make us more savage. My alpha is very strong, and savage, so savage in its desires."

"Perhaps," she said, as she laid her head on his shoulder, "but not as strong as my Igor. He's the one in control. Igor, don't be afraid of what might happen. It's the fear that weakens you. I'll always be by your side, and together we're stronger than either your alpha or my wild hawk. Terry's right, we're a team of our own, a small pack, but still the best, right?"

"Yes, the best by far, my fierce lover. You're right, I'm just worrying, fighting battles that may not come to pass at all. I will forget about this now if I can."

"If you can?"

"I may need help."

"Oh? A distraction perhaps?" she breathed, as she raised her lips for a kiss. He groaned with delight and pulled her tightly to him as their lips met.

A New Hunt

The plane dropped out of the sky to land gently on the abandoned roadway. The hatch dropped open and Jimmy hopped to the ground. Three bags of gear followed then Eric and Vassily. The hatch closed, Clara and Georg climbed on board, then the plane lifted off again.

"Eric, who's flying our plane?" asked Gudrun.

"Amanda, she has a pilot's license. She's a bit rusty, but I gave her some instruction on the way here. She'll be fine."

"You're sure?"

"Remember my first flight in that plane?"

"I remember," she grinned. "Everybody on the crew lost their lunch. So, how did Amanda do?"

"She did great," chuckled Vassily. "I kept my breakfast down and Eric only screamed like a girl once."

"Shut up, Vassily," grumbled Eric, as he stowed the gear in Gudrun's SUV. "So, can I assume Compton is the target?"

"Yes, he's the target. He was warned what would happen if he came at Terry. Mount up, we go."

The strike team arrived back in Boone just as night was falling.

"Gudrun, are we going to hit him right in the hotel?" asked Jimmy.

"I don't believe he's there. He'll be expecting us, so he'll probably be surrounded with agents, holed up in that place where they held Terry and Clara. However, we need to find Terry first, he'll have more information for us."

123

"So, how do we find Terry?" asked Jimmy.

"He'll be here in a few minutes."

"Gudrun?"

"He was aware of me as soon as we reached this city, he'll come to us. Patience, my friends. We want to take out the target, not start a war with this country."

A few minutes later Terry pulled in, parked, and got in the car with them. "Igor's crossed another one off his list," he said. "I've got the body in the back. Egan and the others are holed up in the building where I was held prisoner, Compton's vanished."

"Where would he go? Best guess?"

Terry sighed. "New York. He'll know you're coming and he'll surround himself with extra security constantly. He'll also be working the propaganda angle as hard as he can, trying to bring more scrutiny and forces against us."

Gudrun sighed. "Ah well, in that case we'd better get moving. The sooner we deal with him the better."

"Not really," said Terry. "Americans are a paranoid bunch, especially those in control. You take him out military style and it'll just reinforce what he's been saying."

"And normally that wouldn't matter as we'd strike then return home. However, you're right. If we reinforce his accusations that'll just put more pressure on the Lair. I doubt Harald would be happy about having to abandon that place so soon. However, I want Compton dead. Terry, you know this has to happen."

"I agree, my love. It has to happen, but I think we need to play dirty here."

"Oh, what do you mean, play dirty?"

"I mean, do to him what we did to Krebs. Get him raving about vampires and werewolves, then take him out so it looks like a suicide, cracked from stress and checked out."

Gudrun thought for a moment then nodded. "All right, we can do this. You stay here to work with Igor. Let me take care of Compton."

"Got a plan?"

"I don't have to hide my true nature from my troops any longer. We'll go after him differently now. First, I'll take down those other agents, confirm Compton's whereabouts, and then call Gina. If he's in New York she'll have his location for me when I get there.

"We'll give Compton a few nightmares then I'll command him to write a suicide note before I kill him."

"You'll make him kill himself?"

"No Terry, my love, he'll die by my hand, but the world will believe it a suicide."

Terry nodded slowly. "Be careful, lover. He'll have security everywhere, both electronic as well as active agents."

She leaned closer and kissed him softly. "Rest easy, my darling, we'll take care of Compton. You get to deal with the horny teenagers."

"Lucky me," he chuckled, as he kissed her again then got out of the car. He closed the door and watched them drive away.

EGAN BRIDGER SIGHED as he leaned back in his chair. The other four agents with him were nervously checking and rechecking their automatic weapons. "Egan, are you sure about this?"

"One hundred per cent certain. The woman will be pissed, big time. She'll come, tonight or tomorrow at the latest. It's Compton she wants, you morons will die for nothing if you point those weapons at her."

"You're the Deputy Director, Egan, why don't you just order us to stand down?"

"What, and have you crying to the senate committee that I was working with them? Forget that. Look, you can't stop these people. They're the best in the world at what they do. They'll come in heavy, wearing full body armor. You won't know they're coming until they're in the room. Take my advice, put away the weapons and live another day."

"Traitor," muttered one agent.

"Oh bullshit," sighed Egan, "that's just more of Compton's crazy talk. Sawchuk's a patriot. You've all worked with him, and you know I'm right. You saw Compton. He's obsessed with Sawchuk, it's personal, and he's started something that shouldn't have started. Sawchuk's woman will take him out and that'll save me trying to convince the committee that he's stripped his gears."

At that point, the power failed, and the security screens went blank. Egan shut his eyes tightly and remained still in his chair. A heartbeat later the door was flung open, and a flash grenade popped. The back-up generator kicked in and the lights came up to show three heavily armed and masked mercenaries with automatic weapons covering the room.

"Drop all weapons," commanded a woman's voice. The agents obeyed. "Where's Compton?"

"Fuck you, bitch," snarled one agent.

Her fist landed with a sound crack and he melted to the floor, unconscious. "I ask again, where's Compton?"

"Gone," replied another agent.

She nodded then spoke again. This time her voice sounded like a demon from a distant hell, and it reverberated with command. "*Tell me where Compton went.*"

They could not refuse that voice for it compelled compliance. "He returned to New York."

"*You all spent the night here, discussing the fact that Director Compton has gone mad and is now incompetent, unfit to lead, obsessed with discrediting Terry Sawchuk. Terry Sawchuk is a patriot, and the only man who can keep the forces of evil at bay. You all heard Compton say that Sawchuk is married to a vampire and their children are werewolves. You all agree that Compton is crazy and must be replaced.*"

"You will now sit quietly for ten minutes then awaken and obey my instructions." With that the mercs withdrew from the room.

When the sun came up the agents returned to their hotel and began working on the reports. Meanwhile a minivan with four apparent hikers sped north toward New York.

WHILE GUDRUN AND TROOPS took down the secret prison, Terry waited patiently for the man at the crematorium to finish. It takes some time to reduce a human body to ash. He smiled to himself at how easy it had been. Gudrun's compulsion was still on these people. They firmly believed they were disposing of badly contaminated bodies from a government experiment gone wrong.

Just before noon on a sunny morning, Terry knocked on a door and delivered the bad news and the ashes to another family. This was the hardest part of his job, but there was one bright note. He hadn't been followed.

Gudrun had taken the heat off and Terry planned to find another hotel and get some rest. Gudrun would finish Compton, one way or another. Now he had to wait for Igor to finish the job then figure out what to do about the teenager problem. To hell with it, he'd report to the king and let him figure it out.

What to Do About the Kids

Queen Sally lay awake, her head pillowed on the king's shoulder, her favorite place to sleep, but sleep would not come. "Harald."

"Mmm?"

"I can hear your wheels turning. What's on your mind? Is it Igor and Ronni?"

"How did you know?"

"I'm psychic, remember?" she giggled.

Harald laughed and hugged her gently. "Yes, you are, my beloved. Since we're both awake, would you like to get up and have a snack while we discuss what to do about the kids. I'd like to get your thoughts on this and perhaps a reading?"

"Yes, my king, tea and toast will put me in the mood for a reading. We do need to keep peace in the family." She rose gracefully and wrapped her robe about her. Together they headed for the kitchen.

Elaine was already there with the kettle on for tea. "Tea and toast will just be another couple of minutes, my queen."

"Elaine, how do you do that?"

"Ma'am?"

"Anticipate all our needs before we do? Come here to me, give me your hands."

Wide-eyed, the girl came to her and held out her hands. Sally took her hands for a moment then smiled and released her. "So that's it. I was starting to wonder."

"Sally?"

128

"Our Elaine is a bit psychic as well, my king. She uses the talent to anticipate where and when she'll be needed, and to sense what will be required."

"It's true," said Elaine. "I don't always get it right, but ..."

Sally laughed with delight. "Elaine, you're pure magic. If you'd like, one day we can talk about it. I may be able to help you refine the technique a bit."

"Oh, ma'am, would you?"

"I'd love to."

"Tea's ready," beamed the girl, as she filled the cups then brought the toast to the tray. "In the study?"

"In the study, and thank you, Elaine," smiled Harald.

They settled in with their snack then Sally began the discussion. "All right, Igor and Ronni have mated. Is that a problem for us, Harald?"

"No, not as such."

"There is an age difference between them."

"Age difference? She's not yet thirty and he's got to be twenty or close to it. My love, there's much a bigger age difference between us than that."

"I know that, silly," chuckled Sally. "Okay, you're right, that's not a problem, so what is the problem?"

"There are a number of them. First, his alpha nature has awakened. A young alpha, feeling his oats, can be dangerous. Normally, Illya would be able to deal with it easily, help him, teach him how to adjust to the new emotions, defeat him if he challenged for dominance then help him integrate into the pack."

"But not in this case?"

"No, love. In this case Illya may be the biggest problem, and I fear for his life."

"Harald?"

"As soon as he learned werewolves and humans could mate successfully, Illya commanded all the werewolves to find human mates. He wants to rebuild their numbers as quickly as possible."

"Okay, and the problem here is?"

"I have no idea how the werewolves came to be what they are," said the king, "but I do know how we came to be, Ella, and from her the vampires, as well as Torvil, and Ronni."

Sally nodded and set her teacup back in the saucer. "Yes, they were changed by the exploding stone and the nearness of an animal. What are you getting at?"

"We're all barren, Sally my love. I'm not one hundred percent certain, of course, but it seems likely to me."

"And Illya will have reasoned that out as well."

"He's no fool, he'll have worked it out by now."

"I remember how he reacted when Olla mated with Tommy. Oh crap, Igor is a young alpha, you think he'll challenge Illya?"

"If he's pushed, I do."

"Do you think he'd kill his own grandfather?"

"You've seen the videos we took from Krebs. You know what was done to him and you know how utterly savage he gets when he fights. You know what he's capable of."

"Oh dear, this is not good. Not good at all. Give me a moment to see if I can get anything." Sally closed her eyes and began a series of deep breaths, focusing her mind on young Igor. The king waited patiently for her to finish; he had a long wait. The tea went cold and Elaine appeared with a fresh pot which was also nearly cold before Sally opened her eyes and sighed deeply.

"That is one remarkable young man," she sighed.

"Sally?"

"In spite of what was done to him, the aggression drugs, growth hormones, and more, he still has control of it. Harald, Igor knows what's happened to him, he knows what he becomes when he fights, and he knows what the alpha drive will do to him as well. He has control of it. He's strong, my love. No matter what happens, he'll be in full control of his emotions, that I know for certain.

"I also know he wants to return here to learn."

"To learn?"

"You're his hero, Harald. He knows that Ella, with all her power, and Gudrun with all her training and skills, defer to you, and he wants to learn leadership from you. He wants Tommy to teach him, you to teach him, and he wants Illya to teach him. I believe the problem here will be Illya, not Igor."

"I see."

"Lover, it's not an exact science, what I do. I could be quite wrong about this."

Harald grinned and shook his head. "Somehow I doubt that, and I'm not willing to bet against you. What else can you tell me?"

"Well, Ronni is the other wild card in this game."

"Oh?"

"She already had trust issues, and a strong resistance to authority, it's both her nature and the hawk's. This we know."

"You think she'll rebel against the boy's alpha nature?"

"No, she's completely devoted to him. No, it's her possible reaction to Illya that concerns me."

Harald groaned and sighed. "It's never simple, is it? Why can't it be simple, just once why can't it be easy?"

"Because if it were easy then anybody could do it," grinned Sally. "The gods save the tough stuff for the truly tough people."

"Then I must surely be one tough customer," he chuckled. "All right, I have a better idea of what to expect now. I'll put some thought into how we might possibly avoid utter disaster."

Sally smiled and patted his arm. "You'll figure it out, my lover, you always do."

NIKKA FOUND JUSTINE curled up in a tiny ball, cowering in the corner of her room. In truth, she had to pick up the tiny creature and sniff her to make sure it was actually Justine and not some ordinary mouse. The wee beast snuggled close, quivering, obviously upset. She cooed soothing sounds and lightly stroked the tiny creature's fur.

"Sweet Justine," she said, as she lowered the trembling mouse to the bed then laid down beside her, "whatever is the matter? What's happened to upset you so? Come back to me now and tell me. Come on, bring back my sister, I know you can do it. Come back to Nikka. Tell me what's upset you so."

The mouse began to glow then shimmered into the naked woman. The tears flowed as she threw herself into Nikka's arms. "Oh god, Nikka, I've been such a complete fool."

Saying nothing, Nikka held her until the storm of emotion passed. When Justine stopped crying and lay still in her arms, Nikka asked again. "What it is, my sister? What's happened? You should be happy. Today you mastered the change. Tell me what's ruined your day."

"Igor."

"Igor? Justine, he's far away on a mission, how could he have ..."

"He's mated with Rhonda Stockman," wailed Justine, as the tears began to flow again. "Oh, I know, I know, there could never have been anything between us, he was just being nice to the poor accident victim," she sniffed, "but I thought... I mean, I hoped there could be, you know? I wanted to show him the whole woman, not the deformed half creature. I thought if he could see me, the real me, maybe he would... Gods, I'm such a complete fool."

"Hush now, sweet Justine," soothed Nikka. "You're not a fool. You're a woman. You were injured, hunted, and terrified. A man came and protected you. I know him well, for he is my brother, and he did the same for me in the slave camp. He protected you, made you feel safe, encouraged you to survive. This he did for me as well. For this you worshiped him, and so do I.

"Justine, your feelings for Igor were natural, are natural, and perhaps some of the mouse's instincts are at work here as well."

"Yeah. I guess."

"I'm curious, how do you know of this? How do you know that Igor and Dr. Ronni have mated?"

"I can't tell you, it's too embarrassing."

"Justine, you're blushing. Come on now, tell Sister Nikka what badness you've done."

"I was on my way to the kitchen for a snack when I heard the king and queen talking. I changed into the mouse and followed them into the study. They were talking about Igor and Ronni and what should be done when they return."

"Oh, you are the naughty mouse, aren't you," laughed Nikki. "So, what do you mean, what's to be done when they return? Will the king not allow them to mate?"

"No, the king is fine with it. It's Illya they're worried about."

"Oh, yes, Grandfather did tell everybody to mate with humans and start making lots of pups. Yes, he will be angry. Oh, I hope he doesn't make Igor challenge him."

"Would Igor do that?"

"Da, if Grandfather forces him to it."

"Nikka, what would happen if Igor is forced to challenge Illya?"

"Grandfather will die. Justine, you have seen only Igor's gentle nature. That is the true Igor, gentle and fun loving, nurturing."

"But there's a darker side to him?"

"Da. In the slave pens he killed a man to save me from being thrown to the fighting dogs. Twice Igor himself was thrown into that pit. Each time he killed all the dogs and climbed back out. The masters loved it that he was so strong, so savage, but he frightens me. No, if forced to fight, Grandfather will not survive.

"What will they do? The king and queen, I mean."

"The king said he'll think of something. Nikka, thanks for this."

"This?"

"Getting me onto a different topic and helping me to get my thoughts straight."

Nikka smiled and hugged Justine gently. "Are you okay now, sweet Justine?"

"I am, Nikka, I'll be okay."

"Promise?"

"I promise. You go on, I'll be fine." Nikka kissed her cheek then rose and left the room. When she was gone, Justine curled up in a ball and silently wept.

WHILE THE BROKEN-HEARTED mouse quietly wept out her sorrow, a hard-eyed vampire drove north. Finally, she spoke. "What is it Eric? I can hear the wheels turning from here."

"I don't like it, Gudrun, not one damned bit of it."

"Don't like what?"

"This drive-the-man-crazy-intrigue-thing."

"What don't you like about it?"

"It has way too many holes in it, but most of all, it's not you, not us."

"Explain."

"You always say the simplest way is the best and most efficient. This plan will keep us in play for days, weeks even. We never do this. We locate the target and take him out. That's how we operate. That's what's made us so successful for so long. This will get us caught or killed."

"Sadly, I agree with you, Eric. The problem is, how do we keep this quiet? How do we keep the Lair safe from scrutiny if we just strike hard and fast. They'll know who did it."

"Who will know?" asked Eric. "As I understand it, perhaps a few agents, no more. That Egan fellow is the deputy director. With the target eliminated, he'll be in charge, yes? Did you not already put the compulsion on him? Is he not an ally now? Would he not bury the whole affair?"

"You know, Eric, I do believe you're right, but we'd be taking a huge risk, risking the whole Lair and all her people in the bargain."

"So, isn't that what we do anyway? We risk? Gudrun, you know yourself that if we hang around long enough to do what Terry suggests, we'll be spotted. I have no desire at all to face torture. I'd far rather peg the bastard off from afar and call it a done deal."

"They'll know it's us." she sighed, "and that'll bring eyes on the Lair."

"Maybe not," came Jimmy's voice from the back seat. "There's another option that just occurred to me."

"Talk to me, Jimmy," said Gudrun.

"Well, they'll be watching for us, right? Compton has our descriptions, perhaps even photos. However, I doubt Gina has crossed his radar."

"Go on."

"So, Compton leaves the office with a half dozen agents for security. They're on the lookout for a tall blonde leading a team of Europeans in military gear. They enter the parking lot to see a couple making out on Compton's car. They get tough then Gina puts the whammy on them. The security stands looking at the ceiling while we appear and you make the kill.

When it's over the agents suddenly wake up and find the body, dead of a knife wound, his wallet and watch missing. Their conclusion is, Compton went to the car by himself and was killed by a mugger. New York is a dangerous city; he should have known better."

"I like it, Jimmy," grinned Gudrun. "Eric?"

"Oh yeah, that's way better. In and out. I like it."

"We'll have to disable the security cameras in a way they won't suspect," said Vassily.

"That's a job for Marco to arrange," said Gudrun. "Next cafe stop I'll contact Gina."

It's Not Over Yet

Terry Sawchuk watched the rear-view mirror and sighed. "Who the hell trained you morons anyway?" He pulled up to the curb, got out and walked into a store. A short while later, his car drove away with a new driver. Dutifully, the two agents in the black car followed it. Terry walked out and hailed a cab.

Egan Bridger was enjoying his second cup of coffee in a booth by the window when Terry joined him. "Sawchuk, are you crazy? What the hell are you doing here?"

"Trying to figure out your game, Egan."

"My game? Hell, I'm just trying to survive here. Compton's as good as dead, I take it." Terry just nodded. "Christ, Terry, this has all gone to hell in a hurry."

"Yes, well, you fuckers double-crossed me," said Terry, his annoyance rising. "If you'd played fair I'd have been finished and long gone before now. What the hell went wrong? Why did you people come after me? After all, you called me in yourselves to clean up something you didn't want to touch."

"The director suddenly went off the rails," sighed Egan. "He showed up here accusing me of being soft on you, saying you're a traitor, and ordering us to get the goods on you and your people. Eventually he got impatient and told us to haul you all in on terrorism charges. You saw him, Terry. You saw how crazy he got."

"Yeah, I did, up close and personal. Thanks for getting in between us. I owe you one."

"And I will call it in one day. Okay, off the record, how do you see this playing out?"

"I see you getting a promotion soon."

"Yeah, I noticed your wife left town. So, tell me truly, was that green shit really what you said it was?"

"Yeah, it was. If all goes perfectly, the changes that happened in that lab could, theoretically, create a superior being. The plan was to create a human who could change into an animal and back again. They wanted to create a perfect infiltrator."

"Has it ever worked, that you know of, I mean?"

Terry sighed and relaxed back in his seat. "Three or four times that I'm aware of. However, it's been dealt with. There's no threat."

"That was one of them a few years back, out in Oregon, wasn't it? There was a killer who killed like a crazed animal. You and your team worked that case and brought home some bullshit story, but it was this, wasn't it?"

"It was," replied Terry. "The thing is, Egan, it doesn't really work, can't work. Even in the ones where the change was successful they couldn't control them. No, this crap has to be kept under the radar."

"Tell me the truth, Terry. Is there more of this shit out there?"

"Who knows. Probably. Anyway, we're about done here. You've already got the paperwork on it and there's only one more person to be accounted for. I've got two of my best on it right now."

"Off the record, just who are you working for?"

"I work for a very wealthy man with some serious connections, both legal and otherwise. Not a man to be messed with."

"What's his endgame? Do you know?"

"He wants to live in peace, he wants his family kept safe. He likes his seclusion, and he feels America is the best place to make that happen. I swore an oath to protect the American people from unknown threats, both foreign and domestic, and he likes that. Our goals are compatible. Egan, this man stays out of politics, he's not into power for power's sake, he just wants a safe place for his family and he's hired me, and a couple of others, to make it happen for him."

"Is that how you met her, your wife?"

"Yeah, we met through his people. Thing is, Egan, she's not the most dangerous person in the group. These are serious people, and they just want to be left alone. Keep your nose out of their business and they can be a big help to you."

"Oh? How so?"

"Look, we can see a bit of the future here. You'll be the director any day now. Get this thing under control, and in future you can call me when something like this comes along."

"I doubt I could afford you more than once in a lifetime, Terry."

"Ah, don't worry, I set those fees high to piss off Compton. My bad, I should have known better. Next time we'll negotiate something you can live with. Look, we both know I'm of more use to you working freehand than in a prison somewhere. We both have the same endgame in mind, Egan. Keep this country out of the hands of the bad guys. We've worked together before, you and me. Can we do it again?"

"I'd like to think so, Terry," sighed Egan. "But what do you suggest I do about Director Compton's impending demise?"

"Not a damn thing, just put it out of your mind. You tried to warn him, but he wouldn't listen. He was too hellbent on fucking me up because of that old incident. The man was in way over his head. To do that job right, you have to look at the greater good, the bigger picture. And you have to have some self-control. Compton didn't.

"For example, the foreign nationals thing. In the past few years they've prevented a dozen terrorist attacks. How? They don't play by the rules. Embassies aren't sacred ground to them. My boss says make it stop, they make it stop. You know me, Egan. You know I'd never turn on this country."

"I don't know shit about anything anymore, Terry. I know you dumped your tail this morning, but here they come now."

Suddenly there were three agents pointing guns at Terry. "Down on the floor, Now!"

"Hold! Put your damn guns away and sit down."

"Sir?"

"I said put away the guns and sit down. This man is not, repeat, not, a person of interest. He's an independent consultant working for the department."

"But Director Compton ..."

"Director Compton stepped way over the line. He took a personal long standing grudge and used his office to abuse this man. Compton's not here, I am, so stand down."

"Yes, sir."

"Much better. Now, for the next few days your new assignment is my security. Forget Terry Sawchuk, he's working for us, and we'll leave him alone to get it done. You'll make sure I'm safe while he does it."

"Are you expecting trouble, sir?"

"No, you idiots," said Terry, "he's keeping you here and out of the way while I get this done. By holding you here Compton has no reason to go psycho all over you. Egan Bridger protects his people, you need to know that, and you need to appreciate it. Compton would throw you at me and I'd have to put you down."

"Was that a threat?" asked the agent.

"A statement of fact," replied Terry.

"Oh, for fuck sake, Terry, get your ass out of here and do your job. The rest of you, stay here. Terry, we never had this conversation. You guys haven't seen Sawchuk in days, got it? You've been on security detail."

"Got it, Boss," replied the agent. Terry winked and walked away.

Terry took a cab back to his original hotel where he found his rental car in the parking lot. Grinning, he went inside and picked up the keys at the desk. Back in the car he drove to the meeting place and settled down to wait for Igor or Rhonda to contact him. He had a long wait.

WHILE TERRY MET WITH Egan Bridger, Igor and the hawk hunted. Moving outward in ever-widening circles, they continued the search for the last survivor of the lab accident. It was late in the day when the wolf changed back to a man and signaled the hawk to join him. She swooped in, transforming into the woman just as she reached him, stepped into his arms and kissed him deeply.

"Mmm, Ronni's kiss, nectar of the gods."

"Sweet flatterer," she smiled as she kissed him again. "It's a bit early, is something wrong?"

Igor sighed then hugged her gently. "Maybe I just wanted a kiss."

"How about two?" she asked, as she raised her lips to his.

"Two is twice as nice," he grinned as their lips parted. "Ronni, I found the scent."

"You're troubled. Tell me about it."

"This is a dangerous creature, savage, deadly, and terrified. Worse, it's making changes."

"Making changes?"

"Changing its form."

"How can you know this? Have you seen it?"

Igor took her hand and led her to a tall pine tree. They sat beneath the branches and he pulled her into his arms. "No, love, I haven't seen it, but the scent and tracks tell me this. I found a kill. The animal was only partially eaten, but the kill had been messy, too messy. The poor beast had been torn apart completely.

"I can tell the madness of the kill by the scent. The predator didn't eat it all because he couldn't. He is part human, part wolf, some sort of big cat, and something more. An alligator, perhaps, as I scented that on the last one. Anyway, the tracks were wolf, then human feet, then clawed paws then back to human.

"The scent of fear is strong, although the kill is several days old. Some of the fear was the dead animal's, yes, but not all by far. This one is going to be difficult, and it'll take a while to catch him."

"Why do you say that?"

"I think he either saw or found where we killed the last one. His trail came from that direction. He was headed west and still is. He's not hunting, Ronni, he's running."

Rhonda sighed and snuggled closer before she spoke. "What do you want to do, sweetheart?"

"I want to hold you like this through the night, then hunt him in the morning. I need for you to find Terry, bring him up to speed, make a plan with him to find me again."

"Igor?"

"The beast flees west, my love. I'll follow, bring him down, but it'll be too far to carry the body. I can make it look like a wolf kill, or Terry can find a way to get the car close enough to pick up the body."

"That makes sense. I'll find Terry and we can check the maps. He can drive west to a point where I can find him again, then I'll find you to report in."

"You must remember to hunt too, my love. I need you to stay healthy."

"I will, sweetie, I will. You have to eat too. Promise me."

THE NEXT MORNING THE hawk flew off to find Terry, and the wolf went hunting. He hadn't told her everything about his quarry and how the beast had tortured its victim. "Probably the cat part of him," he thought to himself. "Like a cat playing with a mouse it's caught."

Igor easily caught the scent, although it was old. He followed it all day, but seemed to get no closer. Two days passed and he was making slow gains, but it was costing him. He hadn't eaten, and barely stopped for water. On the third day, the hawk found him again.

Hearing that familiar piercing call from above, the wolf looked up. She was there, making a wide circle to the right. A few minutes later he reached a clearing and she dropped down to meet him, morphing into the woman and reaching for him. She kissed him deeply as he changed and took her in his arms.

Rhonda felt the trembling in him and pulled back to gaze into his eyes. "When was the last time you ate?"

Igor sighed and looked away. "It's been days now. The prey is traveling fast and doesn't stop. For me to gain on it I can't take the time to hunt."

"There's a roadway two miles to the west," she said. "Terry's there waiting. I didn't think you'd take much time to hunt, so I told him to bring food. Go to him, I'll meet you there." She kissed his cheek then leaped into the air. When the wolf stepped out of the trees beside the car she was there, dressed in a sweat suit and setting up a picnic.

Terry tossed some sweats to Igor then sat down with a cooler and pulled out a beer. He looked questioningly at Igor.

"Water."

"Water it is," replied Terry. "So, how's the hunting?"

"It goes badly, Terry. The beast is frightened, it knows what's coming, and it flees west. I've pushed hard for three days and have gained little ground. I have to admire its stamina, but this is taking too long."

"I agree. Ronni wants to try something."

"Oh?" Igor turned to Rhonda.

"Yes, love. Look, it's headed west. How far ahead do you think it is?"

Igor thought for a moment. "At this pace, perhaps three days from here. If I push, I can catch it in a week, I'm sure."

Rhonda sat beside him and passed him a huge meat sandwich. "Honey, the car can cover a lot more ground in a day that you can. Three days through the woods, maybe half a day by car?"

"At least that, yes. So, you think we can take the car and catch up?"

"Yes, that or get ahead of it. It's worth a try, isn't it?"

"Da. The way it's going I'll have no strength to fight when I do finally catch up."

"Are you sure you'll have to fight?" asked Terry.

"Dead certain," he replied.

"Igor, what haven't you told me about this one," Rhonda asked.

"That kill I found; he tortured the creature to death. I could tell by the scent of the beast and the victim that the beast enjoyed the kill. It wasn't hungry, Ronni, it killed the deer for pleasure. It will fight, and I'll kill it."

"Why didn't you tell me?"

"You are so soft-hearted, my lady hawk. I didn't want to upset you."

"Hey, I'm tougher than I look," she replied, lightly poking him in the ribs with an elbow. He chuckled and leaned away. "Now tell me the rest of it."

"Ronni?"

"Igor, don't make me beat it out of you. Tell me the rest."

"The thing kills for pleasure," said Terry, "but it's on the run. What could have scared it so bad it's headed straight west for a week?"

"That would be it, Terry," sighed Igor. "What frightened it enough to make it run so far so fast?"

"Oh shit," muttered Rhonda. "I hadn't thought of that. Look, I haven't seen anything unusual from up there. Did you scent anything?"

"Da, I did."

"And?" He didn't say anything else, just looked away. "Igor?"

"Another wolf pack. They're on its trail too, for some reason I don't understand."

"Would they attack you?" asked Terry.

"Yes. If I get too close they'll all turn on me."

"So, what was your plan?" demanded a hard-eyed Rhonda.

"I was hoping they'd abandon the hunt once it left their territory. If not, I would have to challenge their alpha for dominance. Not something I was looking forward to in a weakened state. If they caught it first, well, I could hang back then pick up the corpse once they were done feeding on it."

Rhonda was giving him a hard look. "Don't ever do that again, Igor. Promise me."

"Ronni?"

"How can I function, help you, if you don't confide in me, the good and the bad."

"I was afraid you might ..."

"Get mixed up in the fight and get hurt?"

"Yeah, that."

"Would a wolf help defend her mate?"

"Yes, but not in a battle for dominance."

"So would the hawk, and this human woman. Never gain, Igor, promise me."

Igor sighed then put his arm around her shoulders. "All right, my savage woman, I promise. So, is there more meat?"

"Nice change of subject," chuckled Rhonda as she swiftly made up another sandwich for him. "So, we go for a car ride?"

"Da, we go for a ride, maybe we'll get lucky. What do you think, Terry?"

"Well, according to this map, we started out here, and now we're here. There's a small town a few hours west of here. We can probably pick up a woods road there and cut this thing's trail there." Igor nodded, but didn't speak. "What is it, Igor, what did I miss?"

"I don't know, Terry, I just don't know and that's what bothers me. The wolves have followed this thing too far and I don't know why. Perhaps we'll find out when we catch up."

"Igor, I don't like the idea of you facing an entire pack of wolves by yourself."

"What else is to be done, Ronni my sweet bird? No, this task falls to us, and we must find a way to get it done."

"I could get a rifle and come with you," said Terry.

"No, Terry, the scent of a human might either frighten it more, or cause it to attack you. No, this is a job for Igor, and I will get it done."

"Us," said Rhonda. "The job falls to us, and our small pack will get it done."

"And so to work," grinned Terry. "You guys all finished?"

"Yes," replied Rhonda, as she began gathering the food wrappers. "Let's get on the go."

It was after dark when they reached the small town and took motel rooms for the night. In the morning, after a full breakfast, they set out, soon finding a dirt road running the way they wanted. Igor transformed and ran along the side of the road as soon as the car stopped. Suddenly he veered off into the trees, he'd caught a fresh scent.

The hawk was instantly in the air as well, and within minutes gave a piercing cry, making a tight circle to the left.

Igor leaped ahead and soon heard the sounds of battle. The other wolf pack had caught up to the beast. He arrived to find a scene of total carnage. Three wolves were dead and the remaining two would not survive.

The beast itself was badly wounded, but Igor saw its wounds healing as it killed another of the wolves. Spotting Igor, the thing suddenly grew a human face and spoke to him. "Come on, boy, come and get some."

Igor transformed back to the man. "Why do you do this?"

"Do what? Kill these vermin? Because I can, because it's fun."

"Why do you torture them?"

"Because I like to hear them scream." It gave what passed for a harsh laugh as the hawk perched in a nearby tree.

"Why did they hunt you?"

"I cleaned out a nest of the young ones. I think they took offense. Now, I've got a question, boy. What the hell are you hunting me for. We're the same."

"We are nothing alike. I will kill you now."

Just as Igor spoke one of the dying wolves grabbed the creature by the leg and bit down hard. In a lightning fast move it turned and attacked, but in that instant, Igor moved, transforming in mid leap.

What followed was a blur of bodies and fangs, blood flying everywhere. The beast was fast as a vampire, and it constantly changed its form. Claws, fangs, club like hands, hooves, and more battered and tore at Igor, but he wasn't that easy to kill.

All the pain and rage of his tormented youth, plus his early training in Krebs death camp, was released in a mad fury that was savage beyond belief. In the end, torn and bleeding, Igor stood over the downed creature. Even as he changed back to human the body began to revive, to heal.

With a roar of defiance, it tried to rise, but Igor seized it by the head and gave a mighty wrench, tearing the head completely away from the body. The beast slumped again, and this time it slowly morphed into a large human male, headless. The head in Igor's hands morphed to human as well.

Rhonda dropped from the branch to the ground, transforming as she did. She leaped into his arms and hugged him fiercely. "Oh my god, Igor, I was so terrified for you. Oh shit, you're injured. You rest here; I'll get Terry and the first aid kit." Before he could say a word, she was in the air and gone.

Igor sighed and dropped the skull to the ground as his body began to tremble. A movement caught his eye and he looked to see the skull moving slightly toward the body. With a snarl he kicked it away then found a large stone. He smashed the skull then turned to see another small movement. One of the wolves was still alive. Igor transformed and went to it.

The wolf whimpered and looked up at him, pleading with its eyes. It was the pack alpha. Igor licked at its face for a moment then bit down hard on its neck. There was a cracking sound then the wolf lay still. Igor transformed back again. "Forgive me, my brother, but you could not have survived. You fought bravely. Join your pack now, run free in the great forest. Perhaps one day we will meet there again."

He turned away then and sank to the ground beneath a tree where he could easily see the body and the shattered skull. He was nearly unconscious when Rhonda returned with the first aid kit. She had tears in her eyes as she cleaned and bandaged his wounds. "It's all right, my pretty bird," he grinned weakly. "Igor is tougher than he looks."

"Hush now, let Dr. Ronni fuss over you, my savage warrior," she said as she finished tying the last bandage. She kissed him softly then helped him to his feet.

"I can travel easier as ..."

"Don't you dare transform, mister. All the bandages will fall off if you do. Here, lean on me instead. Let me help you."

Terry had stuffed the body into a body bag. He smashed the skull into more pieces and scattered them around. "I see you separated the head from the body, was it trying to revive?"

"It was, yes."

"Then we'll leave the skull parts here and cremate the rest. That should do it." He grunted with the effort of getting the large body up onto his shoulder. "Ronni, take Igor back to the car and get him fixed up. I'll catch up, but this bugger is heavy. It'll take me a while."

It was an hour later Terry staggered out of the trees with the body over his shoulder. The cooler was open, and Rhonda was feeding Igor the last of the picnic supplies. "How's he doing, Ronni?"

"Better than I expected. My darling boy heals fast." She kissed Igor's cheek and smiled with relief.

"Can you tell me what happened back there, Igor?"

"Ronni found him, but so did the wolf pack. He'd already killed most of them when I arrived. He grew a human face to tell me how much he loved to hear his victims scream. He was so much like one of the trainers Krebs used on us, had I met him in human form I'd have killed him anyway."

"Did you figure out why the wolves were after him?"

"He found their den and killed all the young while the adults were out hunting. They must have smelled the wrongness about him. They were already down when I got there. I didn't have to fight the alpha."

"Terry, this is the last one, right?" said Rhonda. "It's all over now, isn't it?"

"Yeah, it's over, Ronni. We'll get this guy cremated then I'll get you guys into a rental car so you can go home."

"You're not coming?"

"There's still some mopping up to do. If Kylie and Clara were here to help me it would go faster, but they're not. I'll just have to muddle through on my own. I'll deliver the ashes, finish tidying up the mess, then I'll head home."

"Want some help?"

"Ronni?"

"I'm still a vet, Terry, and familiar with this town and the area. I can help, and my darling boy could use a few days of rest and good food."

"You guys sure about this? You've done your part; you can go home."

"No, we'll stay to help you," said Igor.

"Talk to me, Igor."

"Terry, I need to heal fully before I return to the Lair. I need time to heal, to think, to make a plan, and some decisions."

"You really are expecting trouble when you get back."

"Da, from Grandfather, not the king. No, I need time to think, and you need help. Let my sweet Ronni help you while I heal and make plans."

"All right, guys, I can use the help, and maybe you do need a bit of time at that. We'll lay this guy to rest then I'll report to the king. We can squeeze out an extra day or two before we have to head back. Deal?"

"Deal," grinned Igor.

"Okay then, Ronni, you're driving, I'm beat and Igor's half asleep."

"Hop in," she grinned, as she kissed Igor's cheek then got behind the wheel.

BACK AT THE LAIR THE king looked concerned as he reached for the queen. She'd stopped speaking in mid-sentence, falling into a half trance, as though watching something far away. "Sally? What is it, my love?"

"It's Igor," she replied, shaking off the mood. The others sat up and paid closer attention. "He's fought a battle, but he's going to be fine."

"Can you tell us more?" asked Ella.

"He fought some sort of monster. I'm assuming it was something created in that lab accident. He frightened me, people. I've never felt a rage so hot, not even from Mobutu, but that's not what scares me. Igor's in complete control of it. He let loose the rage as he fought, and shut it off when it was over.

"He left here a boy looking for his place in the world. He'll return a man, a man in full control of himself, his power, his emotions, what was done to him in the past, all of it."

"In other words, a full alpha," sighed the king. "Is he going to challenge me?"

Sally smiled at that. "No, you're his hero, Harald. He saw you in battle against Krebs men. No, I get the sense Igor's in control of his alpha, not the other way around. No, it's Illya I fear for. If he forces the issue, Igor could kill him."

"What else?" asked Harald. "You're smiling, there's something else, isn't there?"

"Yes. I get the sense this young warrior wants to be more than he is. We'll know more once he returns. Right now, I have another concern to deal with."

"Sally?"

"Harald, we have a broken-hearted mouse on our hands. I think I need to spend a bit of time with Justine." With that she rose and left the great hall.

Justine was in her room, sitting quietly, staring into space. She didn't even look up as Sally entered the room. Nikka had been sitting with her, reading. She rose to go as Sally arrived, but Sally waved her back to her chair.

The queen sat beside the mouse and took the girl in her arms. "I know how badly your heart hurts now, and I'll tell you a secret nobody else knows, not even the king. I'd just turned twenty when I fell in love, made a complete fool of myself when I met his wife, and eventually figured out he was just being a nice guy. I read a lot more into it than was there.

"Being broken-hearted and utterly mortified at the same time really sucks."

Justine giggled in spite of herself. "Yes, my queen, truly it does. How did I get myself into this mess anyway?"

It was Nikka who had the answer. "You were injured in an accident, you were terrified, and Igor rescued you."

"Yes. He called me his little mouse, his beautiful Justine."

"My sister, that wasn't Igor speaking; it was his alpha nature. I was his little wolf, his beautiful savage sister. We were all his, his pack, and he protected us as best he could. Justine, what you felt was his kindness, his nurturing, his caring self, his alpha nature. Add to that his poor English ..."

"It lost something in the translation? Nikka, why didn't you say anything before?"

The girl sighed and studied her hands. "Because you needed the illusion. Without it you wouldn't have been able to gain control of the change. Your desire to show Igor the whole woman gave you a reason, a need to gain control. Better to be broken-hearted than to be locked in a room forever, neither woman nor mouse."

Sally reached out to gently caress the girl's cheek. "Nikka, when did you become so old and wise?"

"Last month," she giggled. "I talked to Miss Amanda, asked her what I could do to help my new sister. These things she told me."

Justine moved over and took Nikka into her arms. "That was a cruel kindness, my sister, and absolutely the right thing to do. I hate to admit it, but you're both right about this. Igor's made his choice, and for a wolf that's final. Now I have to let him go and face life alone."

"You won't be alone forever, Justine," smiled Sally. "I just caught a vision of you in a wedding dress. Come on, I think we're at the ice cream stage now. A few tubs of the good stuff and then you can move on." Sally took the woman by the hand and led both of the girls to the kitchen where Elaine had two tubs and three bowls waiting on the counter.

Putting It To Rest

"That's him? That's my boy? That's all that's left of Arlo?"

"We're very sorry for your loss, Mrs. Graves," said Rhonda, as she passed over the urn of ashes. The woman filled up with tears as she took the urn. The big man behind her spoke up. "What the hell happened to him? You people said you'd find him and bring him back alive. You tell me what happened to my boy."

"Mr. Graves," said Terry, "I'm afraid the local police were a bit optimistic when they first spoke to you. It's not their fault, government secrecy and all that. Something got delivered to that lab that shouldn't have. It was a mix up in the labeling. Anyway, somebody opened the package and let out a deadly toxin.

"Everybody who was there became ill and were rushed off to a special hospital for treatment. Sadly, it was too late. Your son was the last survivor, obviously the strongest of the people there. The bodies had to be cremated to prevent the spread of the disease. Again, our condolences for your loss."

The big man seemed mollified by that and, grumbling about the damned government, turned back into the house. The woman thanked them for bringing her son home then she too disappeared inside. Terry and Rhonda returned to the car and drove away.

Noticing that his companion seemed somewhat quieter than usual, Terry spoke. "What's on your mind, Ronni?"

"Way too much to catalog," she sighed. "Igor and his grandfather, mostly."

"You sure it's not Igor and you?"

"So, when did you take over Clyde's job?"

"Last week when he went back to the Lair," grinned Terry.

That made her chuckle. "Okay, that's a big piece of it all right, and I'll admit it. Everybody seems to think Illya will freak out because Igor and I've mated, married, bonded, or whatever the heck we non-humans call it."

"Yeah, I expect he will. He freaked when Olla bonded with Tommy because he'd already chosen someone else for her. Apparently, among the werewolves, the alpha says who mates and who doesn't."

"Yeah? Well screw that shit. My alpha already made that choice."

"Easy girl, save some of that fierceness for later."

"Sorry. So, he'll flip out. Terry, Igor will kill him. I don't want my boy having to live with that on his conscience. What happened about Olla? How did they get around that?"

"That was Sally. The werewolves were under the protection of the king; he was gone, leaving Sally in charge. She gave the okay and the vampires backed her up, so did Gudrun's crew. Look, I've been with these folks long enough to know they'll already have a plan. The king's no fool, he'll know what's coming and he'll have a plan for dealing with it."

"So, you're saying that I should just relax and let the big kids sort it out?"

"Yup. That's what I'd do."

"But what'll happen if they don't have a plan, or if they can't stop it ...?"

"You'll come at me for giving you bad advice and I'll hide behind Gudrun."

That made her laugh. "You're a nut, Terry, you know that? So, you think they'll have it under control?"

"Yeah, I do, Ronni. Gudrun always says, never fight imaginary battles, there's enough real ones to worry about."

"I guess. Fine, then I'll worry about the other one."

"The other one?"

"Justine."

"Hmmm, yeah, Igor poured it on a bit thick with her. He was feeling all protective and we really needed the information she could share. You think she read more into it than was there?"

"Don't you? 'Cause if that had been me, I sure would have."

"What does Igor say? Or have you talked to him about it yet?"

"Not yet, I guess I'm a bit scared to broach the subject right now."

"So, you're really a chicken hawk?"

"Oh!" She turned and slapped his arm. "You think that's funny."

"Oh gods, yes I do."

"Oh yeah, well, your wife may be a vampire, but you're the beast in the family." She sighed and sat back, melting into the seat. "Yeah, I'm being a chicken hawk. So, I should talk to him, huh?"

"Probably should, you know, before you lose control and eat the mouse for kissing your boyfriend or something."

"Shut up, Terry. You're having far too much fun at my expense. Stop the car and let me out."

"Ronni?"

"I'll come back. Just leave the hotel room window open so I don't have to walk through the lobby naked.

"I need to think, Terry, and I think better as the hawk."

"You mean get a bird's eye view of the situation?"

"You're really pushing your luck mister," she grinned as he pulled over.

Terry took a quick look around. "Coast is clear, Ronni. See you back at the hotel."

With a piercing cry the hawk leaped skyward. As Terry drove the rest of the way back to the hotel alone, she floated high above on a warm updraft. "Okay, Ronni, cough it up and take a hard look at it. Yes, the wolf mates for life, however, the alpha may have only one alpha female, but he may mate with several other females to produce pups, ensure the continued survival of the pack. What do you plan to do if that's the way Igor wants to play it?

"Sadly, there can be only one answer to that. Spend the next two hundred years or so alone until time takes him from my heart. Some people do fine in group marriages, some even prefer that, but I'm not one of them. The hawk has only one mate, only one. That's how it has to be for me.

"Terry's right, this thing is eating me alive. I have to talk to Igor, get this straightened out." With her mind set, she turned towards the hotel. It was a long time before she arrived.

Terry was working on the laptop computer and Igor was pacing when the hawk flew through the window and morphed into Rhonda as she alit. Igor reached for her, but she brushed past him and reached for a robe.

"We're not done yet, people. On my way here I saw movement and took a closer look. We missed one. Either Justine didn't know someone else was there, or somebody was just outside the lab and got caught in the blast. Probably the security guy making his rounds. Anyway, we've got one more to track down." She seized up the last piece of pizza and took a bite.

Igor stepped closer, reaching for her once again. "Ronni, why are you angry? Have I done to upset you?"

"Nothing, nothing at all." She sighed and leaned against his shoulder. "Look, there's something we need to discuss, and soon, but first we have a mission to complete. I'll go keep an eye on it and you guys can catch up in the morning." Without warning she turned and leaped through the open window, disappearing into the night sky.

Igor stood staring out that window for a long time. Finally, his shoulders slumped and he turned away. "I don't understand what just happened." Terry made no reply but his face told a different story. "Terry, talk to me. What just happened here? Why is Ronni so angry?"

Terry leaned back from the computer and took a sip of his beer. "Igor, my friend, your woman is afraid, jealous, and angry. Probably angry at herself as much as she is at you. I'm not too sure about this, but I just took a look at wolves on the internet, and I think I have an idea of what's going through her mind."

"So, talk to me, tell me what's going on, how do I fix it?"

Annoyance had crept into his voice and Terry was suddenly wary. He didn't want to be in a confined space with an angry werewolf. He eased around in the chair, making sure he had a clear path to the door. Igor noticed and also noticed the man's hand within easy reach of his gun. He sighed and sat heavily on the edge of the bed.

"Does no one at all trust Igor now? Will Igor be the next animal hunted and killed to keep the humans away? Tell me, Terry, what is it that drives my love away and causes my friends to fear me so?"

"Sorry, Igor." Terry relaxed and put his feet up on the table, taking another sip from his beer and tossing his gun on the bed well out of his reach. "Just a habit, a reflex. You're a dangerous man and you're upset, angry. I flinched out of reflex.

"Okay, so here's what I see going on. The hawk mates for life."

"Da, wolf too, so what's the sudden problem? What makes her jealous? Angry with me?"

"The wolf mates for life, yes, but the alpha might impregnate more than one female of the pack, especially if the alpha female can't have pups. Ronni is probably like Ella and Torvil now, unable to have children, and she's probably figured it out.

"Now, you were all over Justine when we found her, calling her beautiful, your courageous mouse, holding her, and you said you liked cuddling her ..."

"And so Ronni thinks I will ..."

"Igor, the woman is working on a what-if scenario, not reality. Her plan was to talk to you about this when she got back. She's probably afraid to and doesn't want to distract you right now."

"You are certain of this?"

"Pretty sure. I've spent a lot of time with Amanda and Clyde over the past few years."

"She should have talked to me; not just get angry about something I might do in the future. She should trust me as I trust her. I don't understand why she doesn't trust me."

"You guys are all brand new, Igor. Talk to her, sort this out."

He was pacing again. "How can I? She's gone. Where would she go?"

Terry sat up straighter. "She said we've still got one more to find. She saw him, or her, or whatever. I know where I dropped her off. We'll go back there in the morning, see if we can pick up the trail from there. She said she'd watch it, so we go there then start back in this direction. You should find them both pretty quick.

"Look, we both need some rest, and you need to sort out in your mind what's going on for you. Forget about Ronni for a while and figure out what it is that you want, what you need to have happen, then decide what to say to her.

"She'll come back, just be completely sure about what you want." Terry walked out and returned to his own room.

"I want Ronni, that's what I want, just Ronni and no one else, ever. Somehow I must make her understand this." Igor continued pacing for a long time.

Back in the forest, a badly confused animal, or mixture of animals, huddled under a tree, trying to sleep. In the branches high above sat a hawk, silently berating herself, and trying to figure out how to explain herself to her lover. First, however, she had to know for certain.

"Shit, Rhonda, you could have talked to him, told him your concerns, your fears. He's probably super pissed now, who knows what he'll do. One thing's for sure, I wouldn't want to be that poor creature down there when the wolf catches up tomorrow.

"The thing is, I just can't do it. I can't share him, not that way. Yes, I know, a person can love more than one person, some people do fine in three, fours, and more. The thing is, I don't believe I can. It might be the hawk part of me, but I'm not so sure it's not the human part too. I guess I'm just a one-guy-girl, and I need to know that my guy is a one-girl-guy.

"I hope Igor will talk to me in the morning. Maybe I should just head for the mountains for a few hundred years.

"Oh, stop being such a chicken hawk, Rhonda. Get your ass back to that hotel, talk to the man, and get this straightened out. We can find this creature's trail in the morning easily enough." With that she flew away, leaving the creature alone beneath the sheltering tree.

Igor had gone to bed, but he'd left the window open in the hope that she might return. He lay there, awake, mulling over what Terry had said before he left. Suddenly his heart leaped as he heard the flutter of wings, then a cold girl slipped between the sheets with him. "You're freezing. Come closer and let me warm you up."

"Igor, I'm sorry I ran out on you. We need to talk, and I guess I'm just being a chicken."

He pulled her closer, kissed her hair as he snuggled her onto his shoulder. "Talk to me, sweet woman. Tell me what's upset you."

"I'm scared."

"What frightens you so, my love?"

"Igor, I can't share you, not with anyone. Not Justine, not another wolf, not a human, not for a single moment. I know I'm being a selfish bitch, but I can't..."

He stopped her with a kiss, and held it until she fully relaxed into his arms. "You will never have to share me, my pretty bird, not ever. Not with a human, not with another wolf, and not with the little mouse. Terry has told me that my affection for her has given you concern. You are afraid of what will happen when we return to the Lair.

"My pretty bird, my love, you will not have to share me, not ever, for I will have no other but you. Ever. Others will have to make the pups; I'm bound to the lady hawk. I'm hers and she is mine. Dear Ronni, I will make this clear to one and all, including Justine. I have no desire to bring her pain, but she must know I belong to the wild woman of the skies."

"Oh gods, Igor, I'm so sorry. I ..." Igor pressed his finger to her lips.

"My wild woman needs to make Igor forget why he is upset, even his own name, and other things as well..."

With a soft cry of delight, she fastened her lips on his, and wriggled deeper into his arms.

To Make a Killing in New York

As her strike team neared New York, Gudrun changed her appearance. She contacted Gina and relayed what she needed. By the time they reached her apartment, Gina had the information waiting for them.

"There's a few good spots for a sniper to take him out," mused Eric, as he gazed at the map on the table. Marco had clearly marked the man's route to and from the office to his home.

"The parking lot is heavily secured, Gudrun. Are you sure that's where we want to take him?"

"Sadly, it is. I'm with you, I'd far rather just set up and peg him off, but we have to make this look like something else. So, how do we do this? Where do we cut the power?"

Gina grinned wickedly. "I'll take care of that for you."

"Gina?"

"I owe you one, remember? Let me do this, Gudrun. I won't let you down."

"All right, the power goes down, what's next?" asked Eric.

"Okay, Gina drops the power as Compton is leaving the building. His men will make certain there's no one else in the parking garage when he comes out."

"But we'll be there?"

"Indeed we will, old friend, indeed we will." Eric almost shivered at the wolfish grin on her face.

161

"You can't eat him first, Boss," said Jimmy. "The floors will be concrete. We'll need a full blood spill to make it real for the local authorities."

"Spoil sport," grinned Gudrun, as she lightly punched his shoulder. "So, when do we go?"

"Tomorrow," replied Marco. "We're too late today, and I still have a few things to get in place. When you come out there'll be three more cars waiting. You drive away and the others will make sure no one follows. I'll also make sure the street cams are down for a few minutes, both when you enter and again when you leave."

"All right then, we wait," sighed Gudrun.

The next day, Director Compton sat in his office, chewing nervously on a toothpick. He jumped as the phone beside him suddenly rang. Angrily he snatched it up. "What is it?"

"Boss, it's Egan."

"Egan, what's happening down there? Did you manage to reel in Sawchuk again or did you just buy him dinner?"

"Director Compton, you and I've worked together for a lot of years. In all that time, I've always had your back, and I still do now. Sir, you stepped over the line with this one, but I believe there's still a chance to salvage it."

"Oh you do, do you, traitor?"

There was a deep sigh on the line then Egan spoke again. "I'm not a traitor, not to this country nor to you. Look, she's coming for you. She'll show up with that strike force of hers and it'll be all over. Sir, Sawchuk is putting the final touches on this thing for us. Let me work on this, see if I can get him to call her off."

"So, you're holding hands with Sawchuk now."

"Dammit man, I'm trying to save your life here. It wouldn't hurt you to listen. You double-crossed Sawchuk, took him prisoner then abused him. She's pissed about that, and she's not the forgiving type.

"Terry's still here, finishing up the job we hired him to do. Let him finish, close the file, bury it deep and forget all about Terry Sawchuk. The man's not a traitor, but he is playing well above our level. He'll make us a far better ally than an enemy."

"Egan, I can't believe you'd turn on me the way you did. What happened to you?"

"I'm a patriot above all else, Director, and I'm a natural survivor. I can easily see that Sawchuk's no threat to the country, and he's an asset I'd love to be able to call on from time to time to clean up the nasty and unknown shit. His wife, on the other hand, scares the crap out of me.

"You don't like the man, I get that, but you need to let it go. Get a grip on your personal feelings and look at the bigger picture."

"Fuck you, Egan, you traitorous bastard, you're finished. First thing tomorrow I'm appointing a new deputy director, pulling your badge and gun. Get your useless ass back here for a full debriefing."

With that Director Compton slammed down his phone. With a trembling hand, he rubbed at the painful spot in his chest then swallowed a handful of antacids. He was still fuming as he jerked on his coat and stepped out of his office.

Three security men led the way into the parking garage followed by Compton himself, then three more security guards. As they neared his car, the lights failed. The security men whipped out their guns, but a voice froze them in place.

"Hold! Do not move. All security men look at the ceiling and do not move." They fought themselves all the way, but that voice from an alien hell demanded obedience, and they had no choice. They complied. *"Director Compton, I release you."*

Compton lowered his eyes and saw her. She was armed to the teeth and looked like something out of a nightmare. Her fangs gleamed in the dim filtered sunlight as she took a step towards him. "No," he whimpered, as he took a step backward then turned to run. Three heavily armed mercenaries blocked his path.

Compton turned back to face her, and she hissed softly as she bared her fangs. She took another step toward him, and he suddenly screamed as he clutched at his chest. He choked out a moan as he sank to the floor, gasped twice, then lay still.

Puzzled, Gudrun returned to human form, tilting her head to the side as she looked at his unmoving form. Jimmy stepped closer, knelt, and checked for a pulse. He didn't find one. "Dead. Looks like you scared him to death, Boss. His heart gave out."

"Dead? Seriously? Well crap, that sure took the fun out of it. All right, pull back while I deal with these men then we'll withdraw."

Her men swiftly retreated to their escape car then she set to work. *"Hear me and obey. You will count to ten then awaken to find Director Compton dead on the ground. You were taking him to his car when he suddenly screamed and fell dead. There was nothing you could do to save him. You saw no one else in the parking garage. Begin."*

As the men began to count, Gudrun fled to her car and jumped in. It was already moving. A short time later Gina got a call. "It went as planned, Gina. Thank you, I owe you one."

The connection broke and the tiny vampire smiled as she patted Marco's knee. "We were successful, my darling boy. Gudrun is in our debt now, and we grow safer by the day. Fear not, all is well. I'll keep you safe as I promised.

TERRY SAWCHUK PULLED off the road and answered his phone.

"Sawchuk."

"It's done. Heading home. Love you." The connection failed and he grinned.

"I love you too, crazy woman." He smiled again as he tucked the phone back into his pocket, then pulled out onto the road again. "I want a full blow by blow when I get home."

Egan Bridger and his security detail were in the restaurant having a late dinner as Terry strode in. He took a chair from another table pulled it up then sat to join them. "Well, you're looking pretty pleased with yourself."

"I am, Egan, I am. It's done. Here's the last of the paperwork, all nice and tidy, a plausible story, the lab cleared and cleansed, the missing people found and accounted for."

Egan was looking through the papers. "What about this girl? Justine Henley, what's the story on her?"

"Just what it says there, Egan. Justine was found alive, but badly disfigured. You know what I mean, you saw that lab before I did."

"Yeah, I did, and I get what you mean, but, burned in a fire. Removed to a private hospital for recovery?"

"All part of the service."

"Yeah, yeah, so, she's not going to suddenly show up with a hundred media types screaming about the government labs conducting secret experiments, is she?"

"Nope. You'll probably never hear of her again. We've already delivered an urn of ashes to her family, expressing our condolences, just like all the rest."

"You bastard, you've recruited her like you did that vet, Rhonda Stockman."

Terry grinned broadly and ordered a coffee. "It's in the works, Egan, but you've got nothing to worry about from that quarter."

"All right, Terry. I'll deal with it from here and make sure you're never mentioned. You'll get the payment transfer as soon as I get back to New York and take over my new office."

"Oh?"

"Yes. In case you haven't heard, Director Compton had a massive heart attack earlier today. He didn't make it."

"Wow. Sorry for your loss."

"The hell you are, Sawchuk."

"So, you're the interim director?"

"I am. I've already been told I'll be confirmed in the office as soon as I get back to town."

"Congratulations, Egan. You know how to find me if you ever have anything unusual crop up." So saying, Terry drained his coffee mug then rose and walked out.

As Terry walked away one of the agents spoke. "Egan, do you really think his wife took out the director?"

"Count on it. Do you know who she is?"

"No."

"She's a mercenary, leads her own small strike force, best in the world at assassination. She usually works out of Europe, but she's been seen in America several times over the past couple of years. I finally found out why. She's married to that guy, helps him out on tough cases. A word of warning, never piss her off."

"Yeah, they took us down pretty easy. So, how did she make it look like a heart attack?"

"Don't know, don't care. Compton was becoming a liability, using the office to further a personal grudge. We head home in the morning and make nice, officially mourn the director, then get back to work on real cases."

"Amen to that," grumbled another.

Back on the Hunt

Terry had dropped Rhonda and Igor off near where she said she'd spotted the creature. It didn't take Igor long to catch the scent. An hour later he saw the hawk making a tight circle to the left. He moved off in that direction, but suddenly there was a piercing cry from the hawk. She was circling to the right. Igor picked up his pace.

In a small clearing, two men with rifles stood facing a strange creature. The creature appeared to be part dog and part raccoon with a human face. It was crying and begging for its life. "Please don't kill me. I haven't hurt anybody. Please ..."

One man raised his rifle and took aim, but before he could pull the trigger the hawk stooped. Razor sharp talons raked at his face then she swept back into the sky. The wounded man screamed in pain and, dropping his rifle, clutched at his injuries and fell to the ground.

The second man took aim at the escaping hawk, but a huge wolf, a nightmare from the distant past, tackled him, tearing at him and ripping the weapon from his grip. He tried to regain the rifle, but the jaws of the wolf took his life.

The first man had regained his rifle, but the wolf tore into him before he could bring it to bear. Both men lay dead, and the poor creature was still screaming in terror as the hawk landed and morphed into a woman.

Igor was at full run when he saw the hawk drop from the sky. He reached the clearing to see a man aiming a rifle at Rhonda and he tore into them both. When they lay dead he morphed back into the man to catch his lover in his arms. "Ronni, oh my precious Ronni, are you hurt?"

"No, my love, I'm not hurt, but she might be."

They turned to the creature who suddenly started screaming again. To the creature's great surprise, they both stepped closer then sat down. She stopped screaming. "Please don't kill me, please."

"Okay, we won't. I'm Igor, and this is my beloved lady hawk, Ronni, my mate. I promise, we won't hurt you."

"You won't? Everybody wants to kill me."

"Not us, do we Igor?"

"Nope, not us. So, what's your name, my new forest friend?"

"Tanya. You killed those men."

"Yes, I did. They tried to kill you and Ronni stopped them, and then they tried to shoot her, so I attacked them. So, sweet Tanya, can you tell us how you came to be as you are?"

"You mean an animal?"

Igor grinned. "Yes, that."

"Are you a Russian?"

"I was once, now I'm a werewolf. Your changes?"

"Oh, right. It's embarrassing, and ..."

Rhonda slid over to take the poor creature in her arms. "It's okay, Tanya, we're friends and we've been looking for you."

"Looking for me?"

"All of you," said Igor. "There was an accident, many people were suddenly changed. Some more than others. We found as many as we could, some we helped, some we couldn't."

"Helped?"

"There's a place, a safe place, our home. We can take you there. There are people there who can help you, perhaps help you to change back."

"But I don't want to change back."

Rhonda gave her a gentle hug. "Why don't you want to change back?"

Tanya sighed then snuggled closer. "Because I was broken. There was a car accident, Mom and Dad were killed. I was in the hospital for a long time, but I didn't heal right. I couldn't use my hands properly. They kept talking about breaking and rebreaking my hands so they could maybe get them to heal straighter. My legs didn't really heal right either.

"Anyway, every day they came to give me therapy, that's what they called it, but it hurt, a lot. I sneaked out in the night and ran away. I was sleeping beside a building when I woke up like this. There was a lot of screaming inside, and then all sorts of things came running out.

"That's when I noticed what had happened to me, so I ran away too. I don't want to change back. This body works. I can run and jump and everything. I'm a good climber, and my paws are almost like hands, at least they work a lot better than my old hands did."

"You're in pretty good shape," mused Rhonda. "How have you been feeding yourself?"

"Dumpster diving. You'd be amazed at what restaurants throw out. I get chased away a lot, but I'm too quick for them. They never catch me. Guys, can we go someplace else, away from those dead bodies, please."

"Tanya, my little forest friend, my Ronni is a doctor. Will you let her check you over to make sure you're okay?"

"Actually, I'm a veterinarian."

Tanya giggled. "That's better for me, right?"

"You two go, that way. Find a good place to rest and talk. I'll catch up," said Igor.

"What are you going to do?"

"Not to worry, little Tanya. I'll make this look like a wolf pack killed these men. There will be no sign of you left here. We want to keep you safe."

Rhonda led the girl creature away then Igor obliterated any trace of human footprints as well as the tracks of the unusual animal. There wasn't much he could do about the scent. Morphing back into the dire wolf, Igor tore at the bodies some more to make sure it looked like a wolf pack kill then, with the rage spent, lifted his leg against a tree.

Again and again he marked the clearing, leaving the scent of his rage for any other to find. Since he couldn't remove Tanya's scent, he laid down a clear message for any hounds that might be brought in to track the wolves. That message spoke of death. Any dog would think long and hard before following that trail. He then set out to find the girls.

They were in a sunny glade beside a stream, chatting happily. "Sweetheart, Tanya's agreed to come with us to the castle. She wants to meet the king and queen."

"That's good news," he said, as he morphed back into human form. "Ronni, you must find Terry. After what happened I'm afraid they will track the wolf scent. I tried to mess with them, but we both know we can't take little Tanya to the Lair through the forests. We'll be hunted all the way and that would expose the Lair."

"You're right, my love. I'll locate Terry then find the closest road where he can pick us up." She leaped into the air, transforming into the hawk as she did, and flew away."

"Wow, that was so cool. I wish I could do that."

"Da, me too," chuckled Igor, "but we are creatures of the ground, you and me, are we not?"

"Yeah, we are. Is there really a king and queen with a castle?"

"Yes, and they will want to meet you. Tanya, if you're happy in the body you wear now, there'll be no need to change back, they won't ask that of you. Instead, they'll give you a safe place to live, lots of people like us to talk to, good food, forests, fields, ... It's a wonderful place. You'll like it there."

"Wow, you really mean it, don't you? I'll be safe there, no more men with guns hunting me, trying to kill me. Can you tell me more about the people there, people like us?"

Igor smiled at her and nodded. "Da, I will tell you of many things. There are lots of people like me, werewolves. There is only one lady hawk, my Ronni. There is a werebear, he's the librarian."

"Really? A werebear is the librarian?"

"It's true," he said, laughing. "Igor wouldn't lie to you. His name is Torvil. There are humans too, staff, secret agents, doctors, a farmer, and a writer. There are several vampires ..."

"Vampires?" Her eyes opened wide with fear. "Seriously?"

"Yes, but they're not quite what you think, little woman of the forest. The king is a vampire, but not the oldest or the strongest. That one is the Great Mother. She can turn into a saber-toothed tiger."

"A saber-toothed tiger, really?"

"You doubt Igor, but it's true. When I was younger I was held in a slave pen by evil men, and it was the Great Mother who brought me out. Now, the queen, she's human, but she is very psychic. I'll bet she already knows you're coming, and she will want to meet you."

"Are there any bad people there?"

"No. The king would not allow this. The king works very hard to protect his people, and you are now one of his people."

"You mean that? How can you say for sure that's true?"

"Igor is one of the king's secret agents. If Igor says you are one of our people, the king will agree, you will see."

Tanya snuggled closer and laid her head against his shoulder. "Tell me about some of the vampires."

"Okay, first there was the Great Mother, then the king, and Mr. Terry's wife, Gudrun. She's the world's greatest soldier, but she's full of fun and mischief when she's at home. Then there's ... Oh look, there comes Ronni."

Together they watched as the hawk spiraled down toward the ground, changing into the woman just as she touched the mossy carpet. "Come on, you two. Terry's about two miles that way. He's got a blanket in the car for Tanya to hide under."

"Lead on, my lady hawk," grinned Igor, as he climbed to his feet then shimmered into the wolf.

Tanys whimpered slightly and leaned away from him. "Relax, Tanya, it's just Igor. He won't hurt you, but he will protect you. I'll lead the way from above while you two run through the trees. Okay?"

As the girl beast nodded, Rhonda leaped skyward and transformed. The wolf and his companion ran easily through the forest, following the hawk that glided lazily on the soft breeze.

They found Terry sunning himself at a wide section of the dirt side road. As the hawk and wolf changed back to human form and pulled on their clothes, Terry introduced himself. "Hi there, you must be Tanya. I'm Terry." He offered his hand and, shyly, she extended her paw and shook. His grip was gentle, and she smiled.

"Okay, troops, I just got off the phone with the king. He said to find a likely spot and he'll send Eric with the plane to pick us up. I'm sorry, Tanya, you can watch out the window, but if another car comes or if we see people, you'll have to hide under the blanket."

"Sure. It's okay, as long as you guys are with me."

"Igor will sit in the back with you to keep you safe," smiled Rhonda. "We won't let anything bad happen to you, we promise."

"Okay. Can I have the window down so I can feel the wind on my face?"

"Let's both do it," grinned Igor. "We can moo at the cows when we see some, yeah?" The girl beast giggled as she climbed into the back seat, Igor close behind her.

It was a long gentle drive through some rather nice country. Terry took his time, not wanting to draw any untoward attention. They stopped for a bucket of fried chicken and drinks, then found a spot for a picnic. They were enjoying the sun and the food when Tanya suddenly slipped off the bench and cowered on the ground. A police car had just pulled up.

"Be still, Tanya," whispered Rhonda. Her eyes opened wide as the girl's face changed into that of a dog.

"Afternoon, folks," said the policeman as he walked towards them. "You're not from around here, are you?"

Terry shook his head. "Nope. Just passing through, officer."

"Where you headed?"

"South."

"Right. I want to see some ID."

Terry pulled out his badge and dropped it on the picnic table. The man's eyes hardened as he glanced at it. "So, tell me, what's a federal agent doing here?"

Terry sighed then stood to look the man in the eye. "Minding my own damn business, officer. I suggest you do the same. I'm Special Agent Sawchuk, this is Dr. Rhonda Stockman, and this is Agent Igor Hunter. We're going about our business and I caution you not to interfere."

"Igor? That's a Russian name, isn't it?" His hand was resting on the butt of his gun.

"Da, it's Russian." Igor didn't even look up at first. Finally, he made eye contact. "I was born in the forests of Russia, captured and trained as an assassin, then rescued by Agent Sawchuk a few years ago." He slowly rose to his feet.

"Igor works for me now." Terry slipped his badge back into his pocket. "He's our tracker. We've been looking for a certain individual who didn't want to be found."

"So, you stopped to have a picnic?"

Igor grinned and sat back down. "Da, that's because I found him." He took a bite of chicken the passed the rest of the piece to Tanya.

The policeman relaxed his posture, moving his hand away from his gun. He looked at Tanya. "That's got to be the ugliest dog I've ever seen, looks like it's half 'coon."

"No," said Igor, petting Tanya's head gently, "she is very beautiful, our forest runner. Don't listen to this man, sweet forest girl, he's just jealous that he doesn't have such a beautiful companion to keep him company."

"Igor's right," grinned Rhonda, as she too petted Tanya who snuggled closer between them. "He's just jealous."

The policeman sighed then turned away. "Fine, just don't cause any trouble in my county. If you're after anyone around here you come to me first."

"Count on it, Officer," grinned Terry, as he watched the man retreat to his car and drive away. "Moron."

"Bully," said Tanya, who had returned to her original form of a human face.

"Yes, he is," agreed Rhonda. "Tanya, that was pretty amazing, how you changed your face. What else can you do?"

"Promise you won't laugh?"

"We'll never laugh at you, sweet forest woman," said Igor. "Show us what else you can do."

She nodded eagerly then furrowed her brow. Slowly she became the full bloodhound. A moment later she morphed into full raccoon for a minute, and then back to her favorite form. "If I need to climb or break into something I do raccoon, and if I have to run for it I'll go full hound, but mostly I like half and half with the human face."

"Why, Tanya, why is this form the best?"

"I like this one, Terry, because I can run fast, I can climb pretty good, and I can still be me. If I go dog too long I start to think like a hound, and if I do raccoon too long I... you know. This one lets me be me. I can still think straight, but look after myself too."

"You are so very wise, my lady of the forest. A strange thing happened to you, and yet you learned to adapt, to make it better than it was. Is she not amazing, Ronni?"

"Yes she is, our Tanya of the trees is amazing. We'll keep her, right?"

"Da, we'll keep her, right, Terry?"

Terry grinned, but had no chance to answer. Instead he answered his ringing phone. "Sawchuk."

"It's Sally. Let me talk to the new girl."

"Yes, ma'am. Tanya, this is Queen Sally on the phone." He held out the phone and Tanya sat up, holding the phone in both front paws. "Hello?"

"Tanya, Igor's right, you're amazing. Tell me you'll come live here at the castle with us."

"Wow, you're really a queen?"

"I sure am."

"I'd love to live with you in a castle."

"That's great, now, tell me what you'll need. What kind of a room would you like? What sorts of things will you need there?"

"Wow, I get a room?"

"Sure do."

Tanya looked thoughtful for a moment. "Actually, with this new body, I guess I don't really need a room, just someplace comfortable to curl up and sleep."

Sally laughed with delight. "I know just the thing, Tanya. There's a girl here who changes into a mouse. She has a small room and sleeps on a pile of straw there. We'll set up one just like it next to hers for you. You can do whatever you like to make it cozy enough for your taste.

"Tanya, I can't wait to meet you. See you soon."

With that she was gone. "Bye." Tanya held out the phone for Terry.

He grinned at her as he dropped it back in his pocket. "Okay, kids, eat up and let's get on the go. I see that cop car parked down the road. I'll be happier when we're out of this nosy bastard's territory."

"Second that," muttered Rhonda. "I thought Igor was going to go wolf all over him."

"Funny," grinned Igor, "I thought Terry was going to shoot him."

"I was, nosy bastard. Okay, that was the county line. There's supposed to be an abandoned air strip around here somewhere."

He pulled over and checked his map then pulled out again, taking the next right turn. Behind a stand of trees they found the old air strip. Nature was starting to reclaim it, but Eric would have no problem landing the magic plane there. He took out his phone and called, sending the coordinates to Eric. Darkness had fallen by the time the plane landed near them. As Eric landed, Terry called the rental company and gave them the location of the rental car.

Countdown

While Ronni and Igor were settling an excited Tanya onto the plane, an old wolf sat brooding as he leaned his head in his hands. He was at the edge of the forest, gazing across the open lawns to the castle. Silently, a huge bear ambled up then sat beside him, shimmering into a man. The wolf transformed as well.

"Torvil."

"Illya. You look like you've got something heavy on your mind."

The old man sighed and leaned his back against a tree. "I'm that easy to read, am I? I suppose you and the rest all know what's coming, what I must face."

"Ah huh. Sucks to be you these days."

"Sadly, I must agree. So, does the ancient bear have any advice for this old wolf?"

"Actually, I do. Spit it out, Illya, talk it out and have a look at it."

"This I have done several times already."

"Let me guess, you talked to Anna, the king, and maybe even Amanda, but they weren't really much help."

"Good guess. When the leaves fall, it is still my decision to make, my life that ends no matter what path I choose."

"Look harder."

"What?"

"Marlene would say to look harder, there's always an option when the vampire's not in the room."

177

The old wolf chuckled. "Da, easy for her to say, she's the vampire. So, what do you suggest?"

"Break it down, Illya. Look at the pieces and see if there's another way to fit them together."

"What do you mean?"

"Start with what you want to have happen here. Just what do you want to happen?"

"I want this young pup to put aside the barren hawk and mate with a human woman, make many pups."

"Why?"

"My people aren't immortal like you, Torvil. We age, we die. Krebs killed over two-thirds of our numbers. There are too few of us left to revive the packs. Even if we could there would be many problems."

"Such as?"

"Mothers and sons can mate, brothers and sisters too, but if you do that too many times the pups aren't born right, most can't survive after a few generations. There's an old legend of a pack that roamed too far and was unable to return for the spring gatherings. At the gatherings, mates are chosen, people move between packs, new packs are formed. In this way, the people survive and remain strong.

"Unable to reach the gatherings for many years, the wanderers eventually failed and disappeared into the mists of time. Torvil, if we are to remain, we must mate with the humans."

"Increase the gene pool."

"Da, that. I understand this, the need for it. I gave the command for all who seek mates to seek human mates for this reason."

"But the young pup disobeyed and chose the hawk."

"Da. It was a mistake to send him with her on that mission. He should have stayed here where there are young human females to catch his attention. Would he do that? No. He wanted excitement, adventure, and so the king sent him. He was out there, with her and her only, when his alpha spirit rose up to claim a mate. Dammit. I expect her hawk got broody at the same time. Easy to see how it all came to pass."

"So, I come back to it," said Torvil, "what's the main goal here? Is it about dominance, or ..."

"No, if it was just that I could deal with it easily. In fact, I'd be more than happy to send him away to start his own pack, if I thought that pack could survive and thrive, but how can that happen when the alpha female is barren?"

"The question is, must all the pups be from the alpha female?"

"No, not all, but some. The spirit of a strong alpha must be passed along so the pack will always have a strong leader to guide them."

"Ah, so there it is. As I understand things, Krebs killed most of the adult males, leaving Igor as your best hope for your line to continue to lead the pack."

"At last, someone who understands. I've tried to talk to the king, but it's hard for a barren immortal to understand the need. I'm a bit surprised that you do."

"I'm smarter than I look."

"Ha, I've never thought of you that way, my friend. It's in your eyes. So, you understand the problem, what should I do, do you think?"

"Okay, what's likely to happen if you order him to put her aside and choose another?"

"He will defy me, that will force me to fight him. That challenge could not be allowed to pass. I would lose all respect as the alpha."

"So, the alpha rules through fear?"

"No, that would cause the pack to turn on him and kill him, but the alpha must be the strongest if he is to lead."

"And if you force the issue?"

Again, the old wolf chuckled. "Igor will kill me and then it all becomes his problem."

Torvil laughed with him. "Personally, I wouldn't use that as plan A."

"That's why I sit here, hurting my head with so many thoughts. I need a plan B."

"Ah-huh. What are some of the possibles?"

"I could banish him from the pack, but that could also bring on the challenge."

"Guaranteed?"

"No, he could accept that and search for a way to form his own pack."

"What are the odds?"

"About even either way."

"Okay, now let's factor in Igor as a person, a thinking man."

"Igor's alpha nature may awaken and change the fun-loving rascal, the trickster we all know. This has happened before; he could turn nasty."

"Or?"

"He could become more settled, more thoughtful."

"Look harder at him, Illya."

The old wolf sat in thought for a while. "In the prison camp of Krebs, it was Igor who led them, was their pack leader. He did his best to keep them safe, and managed to do that, for the most part."

"So, what does that tell you?"

"He is strong, protective of his people. He's smart, for he always found the way to keep them alive, he didn't just blindly fight the men and get himself killed as some of the others did. Since he's returned to us, he has always been kind and gentle with the others, still protective of them all.

"That's still another problem. If I banish him from the pack the others will follow him, all the pups we rescued."

"Well, you wanted to rebuild the packs. That would give you two packs instead of one. Step in the right direction?"

"Hmm, possible. I hadn't thought of that. Both packs would be small, but about equal in size. I would have a few youngsters, and a few more able to breed with me. If I could mate them with humans, and Igor do the same, in another twenty years or so we could establish a third pack. Yes, it could work."

Torvil rose to his feet, patted him on the shoulder, then morphed into the bear and ambled off into the trees.

"You know," Illya mused to himself, "this could work out for the best, but how to convince Igor without getting killed in the process. Hmm."

WHILE ILLYA TRIED TO think of a way to convince Igor of the idea of building his own pack, Igor was focused on the same problem from another angle.

"Penny."

"Huh? Ronni?"

"A penny for your thoughts, sweetheart. You were somewhere far away."

"Sorry. I was trying to think of a way to convince the king that he needs a pack of wolves who are active, not just children to be protected, but fully active members of his people, working with him, and for him, towards the common goal. The full burden should not be all on him, we all have a stake in this."

"Yes, we do. Care to share your thoughts?"

"The immortals must be the leaders in this, our ongoing quest for survival."

"Oh?"

"Yes, my pretty bird. Our small pack will grow, and in time, when I'm gone, it will fall to you to lead them."

"Hey, there'll be no more talk like that ..."

"Sweet Ronni, you know that day will come. When it does, another alpha wolf will arise, and it will be you he will look to for guidance."

"You sure about that?"

Suddenly Igor laughed. "He'd better or I'll come back and kick his sorry ass. Ronni, you're right, the problem is in front of us right now, not hundreds of years in the future."

"Okay, so let's focus on the now. What's the plan?"

"Both Gudrun and Eric tell me the same thing. The simplest and most direct action is usually the best and most successful. We will pretend that all is well. We report to the king. We announce that we have bonded and expect everybody to be happy for us. The next move will be up to Grandfather."

"Igor ..."

"I won't kill my grandfather, Ronni. If he forces me to fight I will defeat him, but I won't hurt him badly. The worst that can happen will be that I become the new alpha of all the wolf people."

"That would be the worst?"

"I'm the strongest, sweet Ronni, but far from the wisest. I think I'll have my hands full with the wild hawk."

"Oh yes, my big bad wolf, that you will." She laughed, ruffled his hair then kissed his cheek. "Okay, so you've got that settled in your mind. What are you going to do about Justine?"

"Do? Ronni, are you so certain ..."

"Yes, I am, big boy. You went all protective wolf on her when she was at her most vulnerable. You called her your sweet little mouse, your beautiful Justine, you held her, cuddled her, and helped her understand that she could learn to control the change. She's probably mastered it just to show you the woman, to be able to come to you as a whole woman, not some deformed creature."

"Oh fuck."

"Yeah, oh fuck."

"Ronni, how do I make her understand without hurting her?"

"You can't, Igor, but you do have to make her understand, and you have to be as gentle as possible about it."

"Da. I am so dead. No matter what I do, once this plane lands someone I have no wish to hurt, will be hurt, and I must live with that."

"Sucks to be the alpha. Know this, my love, no matter what happens I'll be at your side. I'll support you no matter what decision you make."

"Even if I suddenly run for the forest and hide for a hundred years?"

"Yes, my mate, even then. Is that the plan?"

"I've considered it." They both chuckled at that.

Tanya's voice interrupted their ruminations. "Plane is on approach pattern. Please fasten your seat belts and extinguish all cigarettes." That was accompanied by a howl of laughter from Eric.

"Sounds like the new co-pilot is enjoying her job," grinned Igor.

"So it seems."

The plane lightly touched down and taxied into the hangar. Gudrun was there to greet them. She linked her arm with Terry's and led them toward the great hall. Sally intercepted them on the way and took Tanya under her wing.

They continued on to the hall where the king and some of the others were waiting. Igor noted all the concerned faces. He winked at Ella and she visibly relaxed. He had it under control. They sat quietly while Terry gave his final report. He spoke of how Igor and Rhonda had made an invaluable contribution to the mission and how well they worked as a team.

Harald listened attentively and nodded. "I'm well pleased to have this finished. Our tribe seems to be growing. As a result of this adventure we've added several new people to our ranks. We now have a were-mouse, a poor man who is unlikely to ever gain control of himself, but whom we have to protect, and we've gained a rather unique young woman. Tanya, is it?"

Sally gently nudged the girl forward. "Yes, Sire, I'm Tanya."

Harald smiled as he shook her paw. "So, Tanya, Terry tells me you can do some amazing things, but that you don't want to return to human form, is this correct?"

"Yes, Sire. My human body is broken, it hurts. This one is awesome. I can be me, or I can be dog, or raccoon, and ..." she stopped, blushed, and looked down at her paws.

"The choice is yours to make, little one," he smiled as he lightly patted her shoulder. "You're welcome here. You take some time to get to know a few folks then we'll explore some of the things you might like to do."

He smiled at her again then returned his attention to the room. "Well, I'm ready to call this one a win, finally. So, if there's nothing further ..."

"Actually, there is one outstanding issue," said Illya.

Harald's shoulders slumped. Dammit, he'd hoped Illya would have the sense to let go of this. He silently cursed the old fool. "Speak."

"I believe Igor has something to tell us."

Igor stood, and Rhonda's heart swelled. Igor was smiling, he was calm, not defensive. "Actually, I do. While on this mission, King Harald, I came to an understanding, an understanding of the position the wolves have put you in."

Everyone was suddenly listening closely. "Igor?"

"Yes, my king. Some time ago you learned of the plight of the wolf people. You brought all your resources to bear on our behalf and freed us from the death camp. Since that time, you've hidden us, nurtured us, protected us, and kept us safe, all at your own expense. We're a burden to you, a burden you didn't ask for, but one you carry nonetheless."

"Igor, your people aren't a burden..."

"We are, Sire, you know this to be true, and there's a great debt to be paid here. Sire, Mr. Terry is your greatest agent, Miss Ella your champion, Miss Gudrun your greatest warrior, and Mr. Torvil has become the court wise man. Mr. Tommy is the court sorcerer.

"King Harald, each of these people have much to teach, and I wish to learn from them all. I hope to become an agent like Terry, a man you can trust, a man who can get the job done no matter what the obstacle.

"I have left my pack and the protection it affords to seek my own path, to form my own pack, a pack in the service of the vampire king. Will you accept us?"

Harald was somewhat taken aback by this. Obviously, Igor had seen the solution to the problem he faced. By making this offer he frees himself from Illya's command, enlists the protection of the king, and yet by offering service he willingly gives something Harald desperately needs, a wolf pack ready and willing to help him, not just hold back and wait for him to take care of them. He nodded his approval. This young man would make a fierce and loyal ally.

"I accept you Igor, you and your pack are welcome at my court, and I can always use more capable agents. Terry seems quite impressed with your performance in the field. I welcome you and your pack to my service."

Illya stood up and faced Igor. "So, you seek to escape me, you young pup."

Igor faced him squarely, but fully relaxed. "You know this must happen, Grandfather. I have mated with the Lady Hawk against your wishes. This cannot be undone. If I remain in your pack we must fight. I don't want to do that; I have no desire to harm you. You wanted to revive the packs, so I'm helping. Now there are two."

Illya suddenly burst out laughing. "You young pup, I should box your ears, but, as you say, you have reached that age. You chose not to challenge, but left the pack to form your own. So be it.

"King Harald, the boy is right, we are a burden to you."

"No, Illya ..."

"Yes, Harald, my friend. However, I believe I know a way we can be more of a help to you, and increase our gene pool, as Torvil says. You're sending Victor and Peter to Europe to open and hold the sanctuary there, are you not?"

"I am."

"Sire, many of the young ones who followed Igor in the slave pens will want to join his pack, but a few will stay with the elders. Perhaps if we elders went with Peter. He could use the help, and we could be more useful there. We can speak some of the language, and perhaps we could earn our keep."

"You'd be more at home in your own forests, I know, Illya. Peter will be taking over the Russian facility. Yes, he surely could use the help, and you know each other well. You're certain of this?"

"I am, Great King. Igor is right, we've depended on you long enough, it's time for us to earn our way, to be useful. We understand we must remain hidden from the humans, and we're happy to acknowledge you as king of all non-humans. We will help Peter and Victor, we'll join this modern world, but on our own terms. Is this acceptable to you?"

"It is, Illya, it works for me. Peter?"

The big man chuckled softly. "Yes, Sire, I'd welcome Illya and his people. We need all the help we can get there. Victor?"

"I like it, Peter, Sire. I've seen the place. It's far larger than this lair and we will need the help."

"Then so be it," said the king. "Illya, is there anything else you'll need?"

"Great King, in times past there was a gathering every spring so the packs could mingle, choose mates, exchange tales, ..."

"And so you will want to reconnect with this pack every spring?"

"No, Sire, that would be too soon. The packs need to bring in new blood. Perhaps every five years? That can be worked out later. Great King, this plan will allow my people to continue and not die out, vanish forever. Stephan Kerbs will not have made an end of us. I believe this is the best solution. These youngsters will be more useful to you here. You can use them."

The king sighed and sat back. "Then we have a plan. Peter?"

Before Peter could speak Illya stood again. "Great King, you are the king of all the nonhuman people. The wolves know and accept that. It is the only way for us all to survive. My people will obey Peter as they would you, this I pledge to you."

The king nodded. "Accepted. Well then, we have a plan. Is there anything further?"

Igor smiled. "Only this, my king. I present to you my chosen companion, the lady hawk, Dr. Rhonda Stockman."

"Congratulations, both of you. So, you're a pack of two?"

"At the moment, but I believe the Clan of the Hawk will expand a great deal very soon," grinned Igor.

"So, that's your name?"

"Yes, Grandfather. Your pack is the Children of the Wolf, my pack is the Clan of the Hawk."

Illya nodded. "I like it."

Igor sighed and relaxed back into his chair, reaching for Rhonda's hand. She could feel the tension drain out of him; the disaster had been averted. All was well.

The Fearsome Mouse

It took a while, but the gathering broke up and everyone sought their beds. This time Igor joined Rhonda in her room in the attic. She grinned as she saw him gazing out the window at the yard far below. "Not afraid of heights, are you, my fine warrior?"

"Not so much afraid, but definitely respectful," he said, as he stepped back from the window. "After all, I don't have wings."

"All right, I'll stop teasing," she smiled, as she stepped into his arms and kissed him. "Igor, did you notice something earlier today?"

"The great hall had no servants, no humans, no young wolves, and no Justine. It was a place peopled by warriors. All were ready for a battle. Grandfather knew this. He saw I was right and that was the best way to solve the problem. Perhaps he'd already decided the same thing.

"He also chose to take his pack far away to prevent further issues. Sometimes when two packs have hunting grounds too close together there can be friction. By joining with Peter's people, he's taken the burden off the king, provided his old friend with needed assistance, prevented any further chance of a battle between us, and furthers his desire to increase the gene pool of the wolf people.

"He is so wise, Ronni, his guidance will be a loss to me."

"I know sweetheart, but it's the best solution in the long run. You know that's true."

"Da, now we just have to stay out of each other's way until they leave. When we meet again in five years all will be in the past and the reunion will be joyful."

188

"So that just leaves one small loose end to tie up."

"Loose end?"

"Justine, lover. She was conspicuous by her absence today. She didn't come to greet you, neither did Nikka."

He sighed deeply. "So, Igor is not out of the woods yet?"

"Not yet. Come to me now, my lover. You need to get a good night's rest. Tomorrow will be a long day."

"Da, tomorrow I face the tougher battle."

"Oh, don't whine." She laughed as she pulled him closer for a kiss.

WHILE IGOR SETTLED down for the night Justine relaxed in Nikka's arms. "It's all right, my sweet sister, you chose rightly. Igor had enough to deal with today. Tomorrow will be a better day to welcome him home."

"That wasn't why I hid today, Nikka, and you know it."

"Yeah, you're not really a mouse, you're a chicken."

"What? Why you little monster, I'll..." She began to beat Nikka with a pillow. "You're a rotten beast, you know that?"

Nikka had the giggles. "Yes," she managed, "you've told me so many times."

Justine dropped the pillow and sighed. "Yeah, I'm a chicken. Nikka, I don't know what to do now. Before I knew how I wanted to greet him, I practiced it in my mind a thousand times. I'd call his name and he'd turn to see me. Me, Justine, not the half mouse, but me, the woman who loved him. I'd leap into his arms and kiss him and ... That can't happen now. Rhonda would skin me alive. Nikka, what am I going to do?"

"Go with the original plan, dear sister. Show him the real Justine. He saved your life, step into his arms and hug him, kiss his cheek, and show him it was a good thing he did. Dr. Ronni's not so fierce. She's a smart woman, she'll understand."

"Nikka, what am I going to do? How can I spend the rest of my life working beside her, seeing Igor every day?"

Nikka sighed deeply. "Perhaps there is another way."

"Oh? What do you mean?"

"Grandfather has told the pack, Peter and Victor are returning to Russia to open another sanctuary. Grandfather is taking the wolves with them. Igor will remain here to work for the king. Anyone who wants to stay with Igor as alpha can stay, the rest will go. Justine, I think Peter and Victor could use a woman of your skills with them, could they not?"

"You mean go with them to Russia? Forever?"

"The wolves are going. You are a veterinarian like Dr. Ronni. You would be welcome there."

"Gods, Nikka, I wouldn't know anybody there, I can't speak the language, I ..."

"I'll go with you."

"What?"

"I said I'll go with you, my sister. You'll need a protector, will you not? Who better than your sister?"

"Nikka, Igor will be here, you can't ..."

"I can, Justine, my sister. Yes, I worship my brother, my hero, my savior, and protector, but he'll always see me as the terrified pup he fought to keep alive. In the new sanctuary, I'll be able to be a grown up."

"Nikka, you'd do that for me?"

"Da. Maybe we can go boy hunting together."

"Are you certain about this?"

"I am, sweet Justine. I think we both need to get some distance from this place, at least for now. I'm sure we'll be able to return if we decided to do so."

Justine hugged her tightly. "Nikka, you're the best friend I ever had. I truly do love you like a sister. All right, if you're serious, we'll go on the adventure together."

Suddenly excited, Nikka jumped up. "I'll go talk to Grandfather right now. He'll talk to Peter, I'm sure. Oh, this is so exciting."

As the girl fled the room Justine lay back on her bed of straw. "So, you really wanted to go all along, my young friend, but you were scared to go alone. I can understand that. All right, Nikka, you've gone to the wall for me, I'll do this for you. I owe you this much and more. You're right. A few years distance from Igor will do me good."

IT WAS THE NEXT MORNING and Igor was pretending to be wary like prey, Rhonda was laughing at him. They were just entering the great hall when he heard a soft feminine voice behind him. He turned to see a gloriously beautiful woman smiling at him.

He just stared at her for a moment before he found his voice. "Justine? Are you my Justine, my little mouse?"

She nodded eagerly then completely forgot her resolve. She flew into his arms and kissed him. She then kissed his cheek and stepped back and did a pretty pirouette. "Well, my handsome wolf, what do you think?"

Igor had a bright smile on his face. "Justine, I'm so very proud of you. You did it, I knew you could get control and come back to us."

"And you were right, my hero. Igor, you saved my life and I'll love you forever for what you did for me."

"You are so beautiful, sweet Justine. Now, show me the mouse."

Her eyes flew wide. "What?"

"We are all of two natures, little mouse. You've mastered the woman; can you do the mouse too?"

"Of course I can. Watch." With that her dress fell to the floor and a mouse sat up and squeaked at him.

Before anything else could happen the mouse shrieked in terror as the hawk seized her up in her talons and flew through the window.

Everyone rushed outside to see the hawk disappear up onto the high turret of the roof.

The hawk released the mouse then morphed into the woman. The mouse had already transformed. "What the fucking hell is the matter with you, Rhonda? Have you lost your goddamned mind?"

"We need to talk."

"Talk, yes, I agree, but what the hell was that about?"

"Privacy."

"Privacy? Jesus, Ronni ..."

"Igor and I are mated, Justine."

"You think I don't know that? Christ, I've cried my eyes out for weeks and eaten enough ice cream to turn me into a hippo. I know bloody well you're mated to him; you damn fool."

"You knew for weeks? How could you have known that?"

"I'm a mouse. Nobody pays attention to the small creatures. I heard the king and queen talking about it, so I went mouse and eavesdropped. I knew almost as soon as you did."

Rhonda's expression had gone from stern to compassion. "Justine, I'm sorry, I ..."

"Sorry? You're sorry? First you steal my man, then you scare the shit out of me, and you expect me to believe you're sorry?"

A small grin reached Rhonda's lips. "Justine, I am sorry, I really am."

"Oh bullshit, you're not either. Ronni, I'll admit that, if our positions were reversed, I'd have chewed a wing off you by now too. It hurts, girl, and I'll admit that, but I accept that he made his choice. Nikka tells me you guys were an item before I met him anyway."

"Justine ..."

Justine sat down on the roof and sighed. "It's okay, Ronni. I know this is awkward and this is a confined space where we live. I'm joining Peter's group. The European sanctuary is on the border of Russia and Finland. I've always wanted to learn to ski."

"Justine?"

"I can't do it, Ronni. I can't stay here with you guys so close. That would be awkward for you guys too. No, I need to make a new life. Maybe in a hundred years or so we can ..."

"So, you figured it out, did you?"

"Yeah, Torvil told me. That was a bit of a shock, but I guess we've got time to get used to it." Rhonda sat beside her and hugged her gently. "God, you're a jealous bitch, Ronni."

"I know."

"I should warn Igor."

"He knows."

"Uh-oh."

"Yeah, I got to thinking of how he snuggled you and I went super bitch all over him."

"And you're still together?"

"Both hawks and wolves mate for life."

"So, he had to forgive you."

"Yeah, no choice there, lucky me, my life is blessed. Should we go back now."

"Yeah, we should. Hey, where the hell do you think you're going?"

"Down there?"

"And how am I supposed to get down? I don't have wings."

"Oops, sorry."

"You're damn right, oops. You transform and stay right there until I'm ready."

"Yes, ma'am."

Rhonda shifted to the hawk and Justine went full mouse. She scampered to the edge of the roof then clung tightly to the hawk's leg. A single squeak and the hawk leaped over the side to spiral slowly down to land at Igor's feet. Both women transformed at the same time.

Justine shrieked and leaped into Rhonda's arms, hugging her tightly. "Oh, god, that was a ride." She kissed Rhonda's cheek then turned to Igor. She kissed him again then stepped out of his arms.

"Once again, my hero, thank you for saving my life. I'll see you again in about five years or so."

As she walked away Nikka passed her the fallen dress. Without pausing in her stride, she slipped it over her head. "They're going to Russia with Peter," said Rhonda.

"Da, I know."

"Should I warn the Russians?"

"Naw, let them figure it out on their own. More fun that way."

"Speaking of fun, Igor my lover, you have another decision to make."

"I do? Why must I make all the decisions?"

"You're the alpha," grinned Ronni.

"But you'll tell me which decisions to make, right?"

"Of course."

"All right, what must I decide now?"

"Where are we going to live, your room, my room, or Bill's barn?"

Igor chuckled at that. "I like the barn, but your room is best."

"My room? The room high above the ground?"

"Da, that one."

"Why that one?"

"You have so much stuff and I don't. This way Igor has far less to carry."

Rhonda laughed and kissed his cheek. "All right, my big bad wolf, my room it is. Shall we go home?" He took her hand in his and led her toward the stairs.

Nikka and Justine were on their way to a new adventure in Europe.

The End

Author's note: So, ready for the further adventures of the Hawk and Wolf? Here's a peek at how it began ...

The Oregon Incident

(second edition)
by

Prudence MacLeod

Assignment

The director sighed and looked at the earnest young woman in his office. To say she was beautiful would do her a disservice. Even in plain work clothes this girl was stunning. "Special Agent Larise Parker, how did you ever end up here?"

"It's a long story, Director Bridger," she sighed, as she sank into a chair. "Suffice it to say, here I am. I'm told you have a special team to investigate the bizarre and unusual. I'd like a shot at it if an opening comes up."

"So I've heard." He gazed at her for a long moment. "Why is that?"

"Truth is, sir, I'm sick of humans."

"Yeah, it can sour you when your partner turns on you, that's for sure. You do understand some of the work you're looking for is dangerous."

"I do." Again he looked at the file on his desk, tearing his eyes away from her. "Sir, I'm no fool, I know Director Compton chose me for this department for my ass, not my assets, but I can do the job, I can. Please, just give me a chance to be useful."

"Useful?"

"Director Bridger, the purpose of this department is to safeguard the nation from threats both foreign and domestic. I believe in that mandate, I have the skills, I can do this job."

"All right, Agent Parker, here's the thing. Sometimes, we in this department encounter some things that humans should never have to

198

deal with. Now, I have one assignment and one only available right now, and I don't have a spare agent to put on it."

"I'll take it."

"I haven't told you what it is yet," he grinned. "Larise, this is probably just a wild goose chase, nothing more, but in case it isn't, don't try to be a hero. You go, you investigate, you assess, and if, in your professional judgment, action needs to be taken, contact me. Understood?"

"Sir ..."

"Think of this as a test case. Your record shows that you all too often take the initiative when you should wait for back-up. Don't do that, not on my teams. The thing is, Agent Parker, at this level shit can get out of hand at light speed, and nobody plays solo. It's far too dangerous."

"Understood."

"All right, Agent Parker, you're on your way to Oregon. Here's the case file."

She gave it a cursory glance then looked up. "Seriously? You're sending me out to hunt for Bigfoot?"

"No, Agent Parker, I'm sending you out to discover why half the people who do go looking for Bigfoot never come back. That town, Whitbourne, was evacuated overnight and not one soul has ever spoken a single word of sense about it, nor have the eighty plus deaths that happened at that time been satisfactorily explained. Now there's fresh murders in that area.

"Your mission is to investigate, record, and report. Look, I believe you have the tools for this job, now I need to know you can follow instructions, and that I can trust you. Prove up on this and you'll I'll make sure your place here is solid. Deal?"

"You can count on me, sir."

"Go book a plane ticket, Agent Parker."

BATTERED AND TERRIFIED, Larise Parker stumbled down the overgrown forest road, gasping for breath. She reached the encampment where she'd been staying, but there was no help to be found there.

"Hapoble! Hapoble mon ile pedo!"

"Where were you? Did you enter the god's sanctuary? Did you? Were you within the place that is forbidden? Grab her, we'll use her for the sacrifice. Grab her."

Stones and other objects were sent her way, some scoring hits and others, misses. Now she was fleeing from her former companions. She continued to run until she stumbled and fell headlong over a steep embankment. At her scream, her pursuers turned back and joined the chanting, as the gathered people began to pray for forgiveness and the blessings of the forest god.

At the bottom of a rough slide, the battered woman regained consciousness. Summoning all her reserves, she managed to regain her feet and struggle onward. It was near dawn the next day when she reached the highway, and hours later before she was picked up by a passing motorist who took her to the nearest hospital.

ONCE AGAIN, THE VAMPIRE king was holding court in the great hall. He was speaking, but his queen reached out to grip his arm, bringing him to an instant silence. She turned to a powerfully built man sitting near her. "You're about to get a phone call, Terry. I have a sense we need ..." His phone began to buzz. Terry Sawchuk, once the government's go-to secret agent, and now chief agent of the vampire king, looked to the big man at the head of the table.

The king nodded and Terry pulled out his phone. "It's Egan Bridger," he said, then answered the call. "Director Bridger, good to hear from you. What's up?"

"We've got some weird shit happening, Terry. Your sort of thing."

"I'm listening."

"Ever hear of Whitbourne, Oregon?"

"Nope. What's its claim to fame?"

"It's deserted, has been for over sixty years."

"Deserted?"

"Yes, the whole damn town fled within the space of a few days. Nobody could ever make any sense of it. Anyway, in the past few months things have been happening out there."

"Things?"

"Strange things. A bunch of pagan nut jobs are claiming the old god has returned to the forest. They've set up a camp a few miles from Whitbourne, but refuse to let anyone get past them. They say that town is sacred to the god.

"So, for years now, hunters, Bigfoot seekers, hikers, and whatever else who got near that place just disappeared, never to return. It started getting more frequent recently and thus came to the attention of my department. A few days ago a woman came out of those woods, nearly dead, and babbling insanely about what had happened to her."

"The worshipers smoking some Oregon Gold up in the hills?"

"She's one of my agents, Terry, young and ambitious, but the makings of a good agent. Terry, I don't have the people to put on this. I thought you might be interested in having a look."

Terry glanced to see the queen nodding and the king agreeing. "All right, Egan, I'll take a look at it for you."

"Terry, they're tightening the budget ..."

"Three-fifty each, per day, for a six-person crew, plus expenses."

"Seriously? I must have done something right in a past life."

"It's okay, Egan. I'll pad the hell out of the expenses."

"Fair enough," laughed the director. "What else will you need?"

"Just the usual, badges for the crew, everything you've got on the case, and I want one of my people to interview that agent."

"Not a problem, Terry, but it won't help you. She's crazy as a loon and makes no sense at all. It's a damn shame, really."

"Okay, send me what you've got, and I'll hit the road in the morning. That woman in the hospital?"

"Oh yes."

"Send me a location. She'll be my first stop."

A WOMAN IN A STRAIGHT-jacket sat staring at the walls. She was getting irritable and panicky as the medication began to wear off. Voices sounded outside her door, and she strained to listen. "Has she been taken off all medication?"

"Yes. She should be awake now, but I warn you, Agent West. She makes no sense and gets frustrated, almost violent when you can't understand her."

"I'll speak with her alone. Terry, make sure there are no prying eyes or ears."

"Yes, ma'am, I'm on it."

A few moments later, the door to her room opened and a tall elegant woman entered. Something about this woman exuded power and command. The girl in the straight-jacket didn't move. "Hello, I'm Ella West. I'm going to take that restraint off you now. Do you understand?"

Suddenly the prisoner came alive. She leaped to her feet, begging the tall woman with her eyes as she implored her with inane babble. *Be silent.* The woman froze and trembled with unreasoning fear. Ella West, the eldest of the vampires, took the girl by the shoulders and gazed into her eyes.

"You've been under a vampire's compulsion before," mused Ella. *"Listen carefully, you are at peace. You have full control of your emotions and your thought processes. English is your native language. When you speak to me you will use English. Do you understand?"*

A wave of peace swept over the distraught woman. The panic left her eyes and reason returned. "Yes, ma'am, I understand."

"Very good. I'll remove that restraint now, you no longer need it," said Ella. She took off the straight jacket, then sat on the edge of the bed and gently pulled the woman down beside her. "Let's start again. I'm Ella West."

"Larise, Larise Parker, Special Agent Larise Parker. Oh gods, I can't thank you enough for that. I've got to report. I've got to warn them ..."

"That's what we're doing now, Larise. I'm part of a special team assigned to the case you were working on. Tell me, are you feeling up to it now?"

"Yes, yes, I am, thank you."

"Then come, I'll take you to the agent in charge. He'll connect you with Director Bridger." She rose to her feet and led the way out of the padded cell. A wide-eyed psychiatrist watched as the mad woman walked away. There was a man waiting for them at the end of the corridor. "Larise, this man is Terry Sawchuk. Terry is in command of our team. Terry, Larise has experienced something quite unusual. I think perhaps she should be assigned to us."

"Ella?"

"Your decision, Terry, but I have a strong feeling about this."

"Okay, if you're sure. Come with me, ladies, we'll use the doctor's office for a few minutes. You don't mind, do you, Doc?"

"Knock yourself out," said the bemused psychiatrist.

They closed the office door then sat down. Terry took out his phone and called.

"Bridger."

"Egan, it's Terry. Look, I've got your agent here with me and she's fine now. Egan, I'd like to have her assigned to my team for this exercise."

"Ah dammit, Terry, tell me you're not going to rob me of another agent."

"Maybe, not sure just yet," chuckled Terry. "So, do I get her for the mission?"

"First tell me how you managed to bring her around, if you actually did manage that."

"They did, sir," said Larise.

"Agent Parker, are you seriously all right?"

"Good as new, Director Bridger."

"How???"

"It's a very old technique, Director," said Ella. "I'm Ella West, and I've had experience with this sort of thing before. The reason we want Agent Parker with us is twofold. She has firsthand knowledge of the incident, and I'd like to keep an eye on her condition for a few days. I highly doubt there'll be any more trouble for her, but I want to be certain."

"Ella West, you're that special consultant who worked with Terry on the serial killer case a few years ago."

"Yes, Director, that is correct."

"All right, I can't see any problem with it. Agent Parker, you are now assigned to Terry Sawchuk as liaison for the duration of this case. You will report to him and get your orders from there. Get to it people, there's been another killing in that area. An agent will meet you at the Portland airport with your equipment and rental vehicles." With that he was gone, and Terry put the phone back in his pocket.

"Are you ready for action now, Larise?"

"I am, sir."

"Terry, call me Terry. We'll pick up the rest of the team, then you can bring us all up to speed at the same time. Let's go."

They walked outside where a helicopter was waiting for them. They climbed inside, then it lifted off. As they cleared the city, Ella turned to Larise. *"Larise, you have now joined a unique and highly skilled team. You will trust them, and you will be loyal to them. In the coming days you will see many unusual things. You will accept these things as normal, but you will never speak of them to anyone except members of the team. Do you understand?"*

"I understand."

"Relax and be at peace with us, Larise. We'll keep you safe." She visibly relaxed and Ella patted her hand then turned to gaze out the window.

Don't miss out!

Visit the website below and you can sign up to receive emails whenever Prudence MacLeod publishes a new book. There's no charge and no obligation.

https://books2read.com/r/B-A-ZKBBB-VOXXC

BOOKS 2 READ

Connecting independent readers to independent writers.

Also by Prudence MacLeod

Children of the Goddess
Lady Blue
Fallen Angel
Lady Justice
Lady Shadow
Lady Seeker
Watcher and Warrior
Shadow Ascending

Children of the Wild
Immortal Tigress
Children of the Wolf
Vampire's Lair
The Hawk and the Wolf

Forgotten Worlds
Suvi
Echo of the Past
Survivors
Ship

Fleet

Unite

IGEN

T.E.N.

Nova series

Novan Witch

Assassin of Nova

Beyond Nova

Claimstake

Red Nova

Watch for more at https://www.prudencemacleod.com/.

Telling a story is like knitting a sweater. Start with a ball of possibilities, pull out one small thread and begin. With luck and patience you will create something quite wonderful.

About the Author

On a far off windswept island Jennifer Crandall sits with her dogs and cats creating fantastic stories for all to enjoy. She publishes as JL Crandall, Prudence MacLeod, and Jenni Leigh.

Read more at https://www.prudencemacleod.com/.